Endless Outbreak

Sherryl D. Hancock

Published by Vulpine Press in the United Kingdom in 2022

ISBN: 978-1-83919-186-2

Cover by Claire Wood
Cover photo: Tirzah D. Hancock

www.vulpine-press.com

To all the frontline health care workers. Thank you for risking your lives to save so many, we appreciate you, and you are indeed heroes!

Author's Note

As I finish this book, December 21 2021, the virus has mutated again to the Omicron variant. People are getting vaccinated, but many still refuse. I'll be getting my booster shot on December 30. At this point, 5,380,304 people have died from the virus worldwide, and there have been 275,977,863 confirmed cases of the virus. We aren't out of this yet. I wonder if we ever will be. I hope that Mother Nature will soon see fit to spare humankind. To my readers: Be well, be safe!

Chapter 1

"I thought we were in Europe all this month," Quinn said as they boarded a flight.

"We were supposed to be," Wynter commented, sounding annoyed, "but I guess BJ said this got changed right after our meeting in early December, but they hadn't nailed everything down until recently."

"Nice warning." Quinn snorted.

"It's just three shows, then we're back in Europe for a while," Xandy put in.

Remi and Quinn looked at each other and shook their heads. Xandy was maintaining her Zen attitude about everything. Quinn found it endearing that her wife wanted to try to remain calm in the face of any changes in their schedule, but as her bodyguard, it made Quinn's job harder.

They were headed to Asia, they had three shows in China, one in Beijing, then on to Shanghai and lastly in Hong Kong. There was a day each between the shows, giving them a chance to do some exploring which was a nice change.

"I hate Chinese food," Quinn grumbled under her breath.

Xandy just shook her head, grinning at her wife.

1

Later that day there was an issue at the airport. Various Chinese officials congregated to discuss the matter at length, speaking in Chinese and gesturing to each other wildly at times. Meanwhile, Xandy, Quinn, Wynter and Remington waited in a lounge area next to the conference room with a floor to ceiling glass wall between them and the conference room.

Quinn paced, casting annoyed glances at the officials as she did. Wynter and Xandy relaxed in the comfortable chairs, both engrossed in the books they'd brought with them for the flight. Remington, ever the calm member of the group, leaned against the far wall of the room, observing the conversation going on in the other room.

Quinn's phone rang, she answered with a grumpy, "Yeah?"

"What's going on?" BJ asked.

"You tell me," Quinn said, "we've got six officials in a conference room chattering away. They haven't told us shit. Just smiled and nodded and escorted us to this bloody room!"

"All I know is that you guys haven't made out to my people yet, and they were wondering why." BJ sounded mystified.

"Well, maybe you can get answers," Quinn offered futilely.

"I'll see what I can do," BJ told the irate Irishwoman.

Two hours later, BJ called back to tell them that he couldn't get any answers either. "Sit tight, I've put in a few calls, as soon as I hear something, I'll let you know."

It was another two hours before they were finally escorted through customs.

"They are so twitchy here," Quinn groused as they got into the vehicle waiting to take them to the hotel. She noticed the driver was wearing a surgical mask, but they'd seen that a lot as they'd made their way through the airport.

"What's with the mask?" Wynter whispered.

"Ever since that whole SARS thing years ago, they are all quite careful." Remington shrugged.

"Don't worry about that," the smiling Englishman who'd greeted them at the vehicle said, waving toward the driver, "a lot of them wear masks here." His smile was overly bright, causing Remi and Quinn to exchange a querying look. "I'm Simon," he informed them, briskly, "We've got you booked into two suites in the Mandarian Oriental in Beijing. It's a lovely hotel, very modern and conveniently only about twenty-five minutes from Chaoyang Park, where your show is tomorrow night."

"How long is our break in between?" Wynter asked, anxious to do some sightseeing with Remi.

Simon smiled, "We leave Beijing the morning of the nine-teenth."

"Great!" Wynter clapped happily. "A whole day to check the place out!"

An hour later they were settled into their suites.

"Holy shyte!" Quinn exclaimed from the bathroom. "This place is huge! BJ definitely did us a solid on this one!"

Xandy smiled indulgently, the bathroom was rather large, as was the rest of the suite. BJ had certainly picked a very nice hotel for them. He'd explained that since they hadn't had a lot of notice, that he'd treated them to a few little upgrades.

"Oh my God!" Wynter exclaimed in her and Remi's suite, she was clutching an envelope addressed to her.

"What is it?" Remi asked, looking up from the suitcase she was unpacking.

"BJ scored us a private tour of the Forbidden City tomorrow! I'm so stoked!"

Remi smiled knowingly. "BJ is attempting to make it up to you ladies." She winked.

"So far he's doing a damned good job!" Wynter extolled happily. "I have wanted to see the Forbidden City for so long!"

"You've never been there before?" Remi asked, moving to the window, where Wynter stood, they both looked out. The lights of the large pagoda shaped structure could be seen gleaming in the night.

"I've never been to China before." Wynter leaned back against her wife, smiling softly. "I'm still not sure how BJ did it. I don't think they like the whole lesbian thing."

Remi shrugged. "Communist regime and all..." she murmured.

"I know." Wynter shivered, knowing that Remi was worried about her safety in this country. However, they trusted BJ not to put them in a bad situation.

Being gay in China, while no longer illegal, was still a tricky situation. Gays were still not allowed to marry or adopt children and same-sex households didn't have the same protections or rights as heterosexual ones. Most LGBT gatherings were banned, so being "out and proud" wasn't really something proclaimed too loudly in China. The idea of not one, but two openly gay performers doing a concert in China was rare and Wynter intended to

4

squeeze in as much sightseeing as possible. Remi steeled herself for what was like to be a bit of chaos.

"Will you have enough time tomorrow?"

Wynter shrugged. "Sound check isn't until five p.m. BJ has this scheduled for eight a.m."

"Bondye! He does not expect us to sleep in at all?"

"Like you ever sleep in!" Wynter laughed.

"Well, you sleep in." Remi winked.

"Not tomorrow!"

As expected, Remi was up at the crack of dawn and headed down to the gym for a workout. For once, Wynter jumped out of bed and got into the shower. Getting dressed, her mind wandered over everything she'd ever read about the palace she was visiting that day. She was so excited about the trip to the Forbidden City she could hardly wait for eight o'clock to come. Xandy and Quinn were scheduled to go as well, Wynter was willing to bet her most recent platinum album that Quinn was also in the gym at that point. That thought had her knocking on the adjoining door to Xandy and Quinn's suite. Xandy opened the door, smiling brightly.

"Are you excited too?" Wynter enthused.

"So excited!" Xandy replied.

"We should order breakfast."

"Great!"

Half an hour later, Remi returned to the room, finding Xandy and Wynter sitting at the table in the dining area having coffee and croissants.

Wynter looked at her watch. "We ordered breakfast for you and Quinn, it'll be here in twenty minutes."

"Si efikas…" Remi murmured as she walked into the bathroom, poking her head back out long enough to translate. "So efficient my love."

"That ain't what you said the first time!" Wynter scolded, noting the added 'my love'.

Remi simply chuckled as she closed the bathroom door.

"Say what?" Quinn queried as she stuck her head in through the open adjoining door.

"Nothing," Xandy informed her, "get showered and dressed, we ordered you bois breakfast, it'll be here in ten."

"Yeah, yeah…" Quinn muttered as she wandered off to shower.

"Ten?" Wynter repeated.

Xandy shrugged, "Otherwise she'll take forever. Trust me, her food will be here and cold by the time she gets in here. And she'll complain about it."

"Cold eggs…" Quinn grumbled as she picked up the cover to the plate of scrambled eggs.

"Ten minutes…" Xandy echoed in the same tone, a humorous glint in her blue eyes as she poured Quinn coffee.

Wynter laughed softly, it had taken Quinn thirty minutes to get done with her shower, get her hair right and get dressed.

"Suck it up," Remi commented with a crooked grin.

"They'll be here in about fifteen minutes," Wynter put in.

"I'm eatin', I'm eatin'! Jesus, Mary and Joseph…" Quinn grouched. "Bleedin' tour at o'dark thirty…"

"Wind yer neck in, and feckin eat!" Xandy responded.

"Soundin' like a right proper Irish wife there, love." Quinn grinned, giving Xandy a wink.

During their tour of the Forbidden City, even though both Xandy and Wynter wore no make-up, their hair pulled back and very simple jeans, warm boots and heavy jackets, both were recognized by a few fans. Fortunately, there weren't a lot of fans and those there were very respectful, quietly asking through the tour guide if they could get a selfie with the four women. The group obliged. One young girl stood out from the rest, though.

Her name was Liang and she told them it meant "bright"—her smile definitely fit her name. She told them through the guide that she and her friends were excited to see the concert that night.

"They traveled all the way from Wuhan, because the Shanghai tickets were sold out." The guide, a soft-spoken young man named Bao, told them. "They are very big fans."

"How far away is Wuhan?" Xandy asked the guide.

"About one thousand and two hundred kilometers," Bao told her.

"Seven hundred and forty-five miles," Quinn converted for Xandy.

"Wow!" Xandy exclaimed, smiling widely at Liang, who looked about eighteen to Xandy. "That's a long way to come for a show!"

Liang smiled and nodded when the guide translated, she spoke excitedly to Xandy and Wynter, looking between them as she spoke in fast paced Chinese.

"She said they took the train and that there were so many people on the train that they had to stand part of the time, but seeing the two of you live is too exciting to miss."

Xandy took Liang's hands and squeezed them, "I am so honored that you like our music that much!"

"Definitely!" Wynter added. "Thank you!"

Bao translated, and Liang smiled shyly. She then pointed at Remi and Quinn, then to Wynter and Xandy while biting her lip. Moving closer, she then pointed to the small rainbow pin on Xandy's jacket. Xandy and Wynter exchanged a glance, even as Remi and Quinn exchanged a similar look as understanding dawned. Xandy glanced down at the pin, and took it off, moving to pin it to the inside of Liang's jacket with a pointed look and a smile.

Liang's eyes widened at first, and then filled with tears. Xandy found herself hugging the girl tightly. Wynter joined in. When Liang stepped back, she began speaking excitedly again.

"She is saying that she wished her friends had come to the Forbidden City with her today, but they were being lazy today. That they would regret not getting to meet all of you."

Wynter smiled, "Tell her we'll leave backstage passes for her at Will Call."

That information garnered them a second excited hug.

January 23, 2020

"What the…" Quinn muttered as they settled into the hotel in London.

"What?" Xandy asked as she walked over to where Quinn sat in the overstuffed chair in the living room of the suite.

"Uh…" Quinn murmured, looking a tad horrified by what she was reading on her phone.

"What!" Xandy cried in exasperation.

"They, uh… they just kinda closed China."

"I'm sorry?" Xandy sounded dumbfounded.

"China just put tens of millions of people in quarantine, and it sounds like it's the likes of which has never been done before…"

"That's weird," Xandy commented.

"Is it?" Quinn raised an eyebrow. "Did you see all the masks at the show last night?"

"We saw masks a lot there."

Quinn simply shook her head. "Just glad we got out of there before they shut the country down."

"Me too."

January 25, 2020

"It's here, it's here!" exclaimed the high nasal pitched voice on the other end of the line.

"What's here? Who is this?" Midnight Chevalier queried, as she held the phone away from her ear.

"It's Herbert—Herbert Rudnic, I'm from the Department of Public Health. And it's COVID ma'am, it's here!" the man repeated in a moral normal volume.

"That virus that started in China?" Midnight asked, signaling her secretary Chris to come into her office as she put the phone on speaker. "You're saying it's here in the States?"

"I'm saying it's here in California!" Herbert exclaimed, getting louder again.

"Okay," Midnight said, trying to calm her nerves, they'd been hearing about how bad this virus was, and she had been hoping it wouldn't crop up in California. *Too much to hope for.* "Where in California?"

"Orange County, ma'am."

"What do we know about the patient?" Midnight asked.

"He's only the third in the entire US, and apparently he was recently in Wuhan, China."

Midnight drew in a deep breath, blowing it out as she nodded. "Okay, keep me apprised."

"Yes ma'am," Herbert replied.

After the call, Midnight looked over at Chris. "Get me in touch with the head of the Department of Public Health, I want to know everything there is to know about this virus."

"Yes ma'am," Chris said, standing.

February 1, 2020

It was a sold-out show—with seventy-five thousand seats in the Allianz Arena in Munich and the stage in the center, the show was bigger than ever! Wynter belted out her latest hit song, and the fans went wild. Remi watched her wife from the side of the stage, and she knew that Wynter was getting tired. Her step had faltered a couple of times and it had Remi watching her carefully.

"One more to go…" Remi stated under her breath, her vigilant stance not missed by the show's staff.

The tour had been running at a steady pace since they'd returned from China. They'd been all over Europe in the last two weeks and the group was looking forward to a break. They had one more show to do in Luxemburg the night after next, but then they would get a two-week break.

After two encores, by the time Wynter got off stage she practically fell into Remi's arms in her exhaustion.

"Cheri?" Remi queried as she lifted Wynter up.

"Mmm?" Wynter murmured, her head against Remi's shoulder.

"I'm taking her back to the hotel now," Remi told the stage manager, even as Xandy started her show. "I'll send the car back for Xandy and Quinn."

"What's on now?" Quinn asked into Remi's earpiece.

"Wynter's exhausted, I'm taking her back," Remi told her.

"Got it!" Quinn responded.

Back at the hotel, Remi ordered some hot tea from room service for Wynter and helped her to the bathroom so she could change out of her stage clothes.

"How is it going in there?" Remi asked, hovering outside the bathroom door.

Wynter sat at the vanity in the huge bathroom, she'd managed to take off her jacket and kick off the boots she wore. She shook her head miserably, every muscle in her body protesting the idea of moving anymore.

"I can't..." she said quietly.

Remi poked her head inside the bathroom, then moved to kneel in front of her wife.

"Okay, I have you," Remi told her, helping Wynter undress the rest of the way. "I am going to run the tub so you can soak. I will be right back."

By the time the tub was filled with steaming water and lavender scented bubbles, Remi carried Wynter to the tub and lowered her gently into the water.

"Thank you…" Wynter sighed. "I'm okay…" she continued weakly.

"I know," Remi assured her, but knowing that Wynter would only use energy arguing with her if she didn't agree.

"Just one more show…" Wynter stated.

"I know," Remi repeated.

Wynter narrowed her blue eyes at her wife. "You know I hate it when you humor me."

"I know." Remi's lips curled in a grin.

Wynter flicked water at her stubborn wife, but then leaned back and sighed loudly. "I think I'm getting old!"

"Why?"

"Because I used to be able to do tours like this for weeks at a time with no problem."

"There have been time changes, and your show is longer this time around," Remi reasoned.

Wynter pressed her lips together consideration. "Maybe." She tilted her head at Remi, who sat on the end of the marble enclosure for the tub. "You don't have to babysit me you know."

"I am sitting and conversating with my wife, is there something wrong with that?"

"You really think you're slick, don't you?" Wynter chuckled.

"Mwen kwe mwen entelijan," Remi muttered as there was a knock on the hotel door. "That would be the tea," she explained as she stood and left the room.

"I mostly understood that!" Wynter called after her.

Remi grinned to herself in the other room, she knew teaching her wife creole had been a bad idea.

The next morning Wynter felt completely drained, even after a good night's sleep.

"Just let me sleep until we need to leave for Luxembourg," Wynter told Remi.

Remi frowned, not sure that would do much good. She was right: four hours later, Wynter was still completely wiped out.

"What can we do?" Remi asked BJ on the phone.

BJ Sparks blew his breath out, shaking his head at his end of the line. "She doesn't think she can push through it?"

"Brenden, she is exhausted. She cannot even get out of bed. I do not think she can do it."

BJ grimaced, hating to cancel a show with such short notice. "Let me see what I can do."

Half an hour later, Wynter dragged herself out of bed. "I didn't say to cancel the damned show!" she yelled as she pulled on clothes. "Tell the bus we'll be there in ten minutes!"

"Not sure if we will make it in time," Remi told her.

Wynter gave her a dangerous look. "I don't cancel shows!" she exclaimed, running a brush through her hair. "Let's go."

Remi shook her head. Fortunately, they'd packed the night before, so they were ready to leave. Wynter slept on the bus the entire six hours it took to get there. BJ had been called so he could stop looking for a replacement act, to Remi's annoyance the Irishman sounded relieved.

The show that night in Luxembourg had Remi on pins and needles. She stood in a state of complete awareness of her wife's every movement. It was obvious to Remi that Wynter was far from vibrant, but fortunately her fans didn't seem to notice. When Wynter's set was over they clamored for more, and despite Remi shaking her head vehemently, Wynter relented, launching into one of her older songs named "Fighter". Halfway into the song, it was obvious she was struggling: at one point she simply sat on one of the lower amplifiers, doing her best to belt out the lyrics. In the last verse, she stood and move toward Remi's side of the stage. Remi felt a sense of dread settle over her, causing her to step forward and onto the stage. The crowd went wild seeing her standing there and mistook her rapt attention on Wynter as part of the act. Remi was dressed in all black and, as always, she made a striking figure, but she wasn't paying attention to anything other than Wynter.

Wynter saw Remi standing on stage but didn't register what it meant. Her body felt so heavy at that moment. *Why do I feel so weird?* was the last thing to occur to her as everything started to go black. "Rem…" she breathed into the microphone in front of her lips as she started to crumple. By the time Remi had darted forward to catch her, she was unconscious.

Remi pulled the headset off Wynter and handed it to the tech who had rushed forward to assist. She lifted Wynter in her arms and carried her offstage as the backing band played on. The fans were momentarily stunned, but then began to cheer, thinking it was somehow a portrayal of the time Remi caught Wynter falling from some scaffolding onstage. Quinn moved across the stage to assist Remi, creating another cheer to go up from the crowd. The Irishwoman was also well known from her heroics as Xandy's bodyguard. Quinn ignored the cheers and made her way to Remi's side.

"Is she out?" Quinn asked.

Remi nodded, moving off stage as quickly as she could.

Wynter woke slowly, feeling like she was trying to maneuver through mud. Her eyelids felt heavy, and her thoughts were like tissue paper. Every time she tried to remember where she was or what had happened, she'd grasp at a thought and it would simply tear away, leaving her trying to find another memory to piece it together with.

In her frustration to emerge from the darkness of her fragmented thoughts, she grunted. She felt the coolness of a hand on her cheek at that moment and forced her eyes open. Staring back into her eyes were the kind brown eyes of her wife. Remi sat in a chair right next to the hospital bed Wynter lay in and she had lowered her head to await her wife's gaze.

Feeling Remi's hand stroke her cheek, Wynter sighed.

"Hi…" Wynter breathed weakly.

"Hello." Remi smiled softly, the worry in her eyes lingering like shadows.

Wynter wanted to reach up and touch Remi's hand to try and reassure her, but her arm wouldn't move at first. When she finally shifted enough to move it, it felt like it was made of lead.

"What…?" she began, not sure what was happening.

"It is okay, my love, the doctor says you are suffering from exhaustion, and you just need to rest," Remi assured.

Wynter nodded slowly, her eye lids already drooping again.

"Sleep honey," Remi encouraged.

"You'll stay?"

"I will always be here for you," Remi told her.

Wynter sighed and allowed her eyes to drift closed again. Remi stood as the nurse walked in the room, followed by Quinn.

"How is she?" Quinn asked as the nurse busily checked Wynter's vitals.

"The doctor says she's exhausted," Remi related, "he said she might have a touch of the flu too."

Quinn's lips twitched, worried that it was more than that, but didn't want to put that thought to words. She'd come to think, much like Remi, that putting things out into the ether often made them reality.

Remi took note of the look in her friend's eyes, but pointedly didn't comment on it—she too was worried about Wynter.

"I want to get her back to London tonight," Remi told Quinn, "BJ rented a flat for us to stay in, so Wynter can get better."

"It better have two bedrooms," Quinn commented darkly.

16

Remi grinned. "Two masters as a matter of fact," she told the Irishwoman, secretly pleased that Quinn and Xandy weren't looking to distance themselves from Wynter's illness. It somehow seemed to give her courage.

There'd been so much said about this virus that had originated in China, only seven hundred and forty-five miles from where they'd been. In fact, the young lady they'd hugged and been around had been from Wuhan, the apparent epicenter of the virus. It was a prominent thought for everyone, even if they weren't talking about it.

February 14, 2020
Rome, Italy

"They're beautiful!" Riley proclaimed, as she stared down at the two-dozen long stem red roses she'd received via room service.

"Did you look inside them?" Legend prompted, as she leaned against the far wall of the editing booth.

"What did you do..." Riley murmured as she reached between the scarlet blooms, finding a small box.

"Just a little something I picked up," Legend smiled softly, her eyes sparkling as she pictured Riley's expression on the other end of the line.

Opening the box, Riley saw a beautiful Le Vian cocktail ring nestled inside. The ring was made of rose gold, with chocolate diamonds on the slanted band, and two beautiful scarlet red stones on separate bands. These stones were offset with more chocolate and white diamonds. It was a spectacular piece.

"Oh Legend, it's so gorgeous!" Riley breathed as she bit her lip, tears glazing her eyes. "Thank you."

Legend Azaria was no slouch when it came to showing her love, and Riley found that she couldn't believe she'd ever gotten so luck as to find the enigmatic movie director. As a spouse, Legend was attentive, supportive and always very loving with her. Gone was the overly intense, easily angered addict Legend had been, she constantly amazed Riley. Having been in relationships with men for all her adult life, Riley reveled in the important romantic differences between men and women. The men she'd dated had never satisfied her intellectually and rarely could hold her interest for long. But Legend had captured her attention, then her heart and finally her very soul. Riley had never given so much to one person, being open and honest about everything, never holding back things she thought or wanted. It was a refreshing change this late in her life.

"Happy Valentine's Day babe," Legend's voice held the serene lilt she got when she spoke to her wife. It was something the others in the editing booth noticed, grinning to each other. "So, how's it going there?"

Riley sighed, sitting down in the chair in the living area of her hotel suite, looking out over the city of Rome. "Slowly!" she complained. "The director is all over the place, first he wants us to do it this way, then he wants to try it that way..." Riley flapped her hand in the air, mentally dismissing the man. "I'm sick of it already. He needs to know what he wants going in."

Legend smiled indulgently on her end of the line. "Sometimes the actors give a director inspiration to try new things, honey.

Give him some semblance of a break. He's never worked with an actress of your caliber; he's probably trying to make sure he doesn't screw this up."

"Sure, give me to a new kid in town…" Riley grumbled.

"You wanted to do this movie babe; you loved the script." Legend reminded her gently.

"But you said he was good," Riley accused.

"He is good!" Legend insisted. "You just have to let him get his groove in there, okay? Give it some time."

On her end, Riley made a face, but knew that Legend was right. Dan Geno was an up-and-coming director, much like Legend had been years before. Dan, a member of the LGBTQ community, had approached Legend with the script for the movie he wanted to do. He knew that Legend was all about promoting LGBTQ ideas and artists in the movie business. Legend had been the one to give Riley the script to read, feeling that the part Dan wanted Riley to play (a woman trying to understand her husband's coming out journey) was perfect for Riley. Legend also knew that Riley's big box office name would give the movie a boost at the theaters and Riley an opportunity to stretch her range as an actress.

"Fine," Riley surrendered, "how is the editing going?"

Legend was in the middle of edits for her latest movie, a piece based loosely on Shenin and Tyler's love story, another opportunity to illustrate the effects of Don't Ask Don't Tell.

"It's going…" Legend commented, rolling her eyes as she did. "I'm worried I'm going to need to head back to Maryland and Alaska to reshoot some scenes though. I didn't get what I wanted, exactly."

"Well, that would suck," Riley stated flatly.

"I know," Legend agreed, "but you're not here anyway, so what's a couple of more months?"

"You were supposed to be wrapping up so you could come see me in Rome, remember?"

"I know, and I will, but you know how I am…"

"Yes, I know how you are," Riley assured her, "everything has to feel right."

Legend smiled, it made her obscenely happy that Riley understood her so well. It was great to finally have a partner who understood not only the film industry, but a deep passion for making movies that impacted people. So many others Legend had dated in the past couldn't understand statements like "I need people to be able to taste the sand, I need to smell the salt air." Riley, however, got it and Legend loved her for it.

After hanging up, Riley got dressed and headed out for her daily run, then it was over to the studio for hair and makeup. It was five in the morning in Italy, and Riley knew she'd caught Legend still in the editing studio at eight at night in Los Angeles. Shaking her head as she put on her headphones, she left the hotel. She was staying at the Palazzo Manfredi in the heart of old Rome. She absolutely loved the location. Her bedroom overlooked the ruins of the Colosseum. She'd spent many hours walking the streets, wearing a hat and sunglasses of course, to soak up the atmosphere. She loved the old world feel to not only the cobblestone streets, but the cafés and random ancient ruins that lay about the city. To Riley, Rome was always a wonder to behold. Its busy streets were dotted with fenced areas that featured excavated Roman ruins and it always amazed her.

As she jogged along, though, she frowned. She'd truly hoped to be sharing these sights with Legend in a month or so, but that didn't sound like it was going to happen now. She'd always felt like that she and Legend were a good fit, because they were both in the movie business. It was natural for them to understand each other's hectic schedules when filming or editing. Sadly, it was something completely different to experience the disappointment of Legend needing to do what she needed to do to complete her film Running faster, Riley was determined not to let Legend's change in plans spoil her day.

Why am I so upset? Riley wondered to herself; it wasn't like she hadn't been disappointed by a partner before. Her string of relationships were littered with disenchantments. The fact was Legend rarely let her down, and deserved understanding in this situation. Legend's movies were her passion, and they'd earned her the accolades she richly deserved. Riley couldn't argue with that. It just didn't make it easy to take all the time.

She was deep in reflection by the time she made the twenty-minute run to the market at Piazza Campo de'Fiori, a farmers' market of sorts, that she liked to buy fresh fruits and vegetables every morning. As usual, if people recognized her, they didn't make a fuss. They would smile at her, take her hand, and sometimes ask for a picture. Riley felt comfortable in the company of such warm people, and it was one of her daily routines that she loved.

By the time she got back to the hotel to shower and change, she'd resolved to put her unhappiness aside. She loved Legend, and that meant loving her for all her faults and passions. The rest of her day was spent mired in production issues and reading through scenes over and over again until the director found the direction he wanted the scene to go in. Riley fell into bed exhausted, not thinking another thing about the fact that it was Valentine's Day.

Singapore

"What is all that noise?" Parker asked, trying to hear Talon on the other end of the phone.

"Fireworks," Talon shieled her eyes against the bright display of lights, "they're really into them here. It's beautiful, but damned loud!"

"Why don't you just call me back when you get back to your hotel?" Parker told her.

"It'll be a couple more hours, won't you be at work by then?"

Parker glanced at her watch; it was seven a.m. in Los Angeles. "Yeah, I will. Look just try to call me tonight, or when you can."

"Okay," Talon muttered, feeling dejected. She'd been in Singapore for three weeks now and she was really ready to go home, but her good will tour had a few more stops.

"I'm sorry, honey." Parker sighed, knowing that she was disappointing her girlfriend.

"It's okay, I just miss you so much." Talon moved to a corner of a building so she could talk and hear better.

22

"I miss you too, so does Ginny. When she and Kim come over she keeps wandering around the house saying 'tawon?'. It's really cute, but sad at the same time, ya know?"

Talon felt tears sting the backs of her eyelids, now she really missed home. She nodded, afraid to speak because then Parker would know she was crying.

"Don't do that…" Parker winced, knowing what was happening on the other end of the line. "I didn't tell you that to make you cry."

"I know," Talon managed, "I just want to be there."

"What, like three more weeks, right? Then you'll be home."

"Yep!" Talon affirmed.

"Do you think you could call me tomorrow around ten a.m. your time?" Parker asked.

Talon thought about her schedule for the following morning. "I will make sure to."

"Let's video chat, I'll have Ginny with me."

"That's perfect," Talon bit her lip, "thank you Parker."

"For what?" Parker queried.

"For being you, for knowing what I need right now." Talon sighed.

On her end, Parker smiled. Her relationship with Talon was definitely different. Talon was very independent and wanted her life the way it was. At the same time, though, Talon enjoyed the feeling of family she got from Parker and her daughter Kim, and Kim's daughter Ginny. Parker always sensed the war of Talon's desire to be free, but at the same time the longing to be in a safe and happy place. It was Parker's way of letting Talon be who she was. She waited for her to come back, and Talon always did.

February 15, 2020

Memphis Lassister made her way through the grocery store, practically dancing her way down the aisles, her ever present Bose headphones placed firmly in her ears, music blasting. She made quite the sight with her black skinny jeans, ripped at the knees, her black hoodie and her black combat boots. The only color present were the shocking blue streaks against her spiky, messy white-blonde hair. It was obvious she was in her own world as she reached for pasta, but not before executing a spin in the aisle as the whimsy overtook her. Not aware of any of the stares or comments from passersby, Memphis just continued on her way, the occasional dance move breaking out randomly as she mouthed whatever words went to the songs in her ears.

"The brightest things fade the fastest!" screamed in her ear. She didn't even notice the young woman walking up to her, until the woman literally grabbed her hand. Memphis looked up startled as she pulled her hand away to reach up and pop a headphone out of her ear. "I'm sorry?" she asked as the woman stared at her expectantly.

"You're Memphis Lassiter, aren't you?" the young woman repeated.

Memphis stood open mouthed for a long moment, her blue eyes darting around the aisle, looking for an escape. The woman grabbed her hand again. "I just can't believe it's you, I so loved your album!" The woman enthused undaunted, putting her other hand out to clasp Memphis' hand between her two hands now.

Memphis nodded, mustering a smile. She really hated this, but she knew that it was the price of 'fame'; it was why she wasn't making anymore albums, but that didn't seem to stop people from approaching her randomly.

"Thank you," Memphis told her, nodding to the woman.

"When is your next album coming out? I'm totally downloading it the minute it comes out!"

"I don't really know," Memphis began hesitantly, trying to disengage her hand from the woman's grasp. "I need to, um… I need to—"

"Let the young lady go," said a strong voice from behind them. Memphis glanced over her shoulders, surprised to see John Machiavelli there.

The woman stared up at John with shock written all over her face, but she didn't relinquish Memphis' hand, so John reached over and put his hand on the woman's arm.

"Please, let her go, ma'am." John said again, his voice stronger now and his eyes flinty with determination.

Finally, the woman let go of Memphis, and Memphis immediately stepped closer to John.

"I'm… I'm sorry," the woman said, looking embarrassed.

"It's okay," Memphis assured her, even as she felt her insides quiver a bit. She knew it was silly, but she still had issues with people grabbing her.

The woman finally wandered away, and Memphis breathed an exaggerated sigh of relief.

"You okay?" John asked.

"Yeah, I just… you know…"

"I know." John nodded his head.

Everyone knew that Memphis was still traumatized by her time with the cult that had almost cost her her life. She didn't need to explain. John, who happened to be at the same store, had been just about to say something to Memphis when he'd seen the woman approach. He's also seen the look on Memphis' face when the woman had grabbed at her, but he'd stayed out of it until he knew that Memphis was on the verge of panic.

"Thanks Mackie." Memphis still looked affected by the situation, but John knew she was doing her best to hide it.

He chucked her on the shoulder. "Any time, little one." He winked and sauntered away.

Memphis finished her shopping quickly and checked out through self-check-out to avoid dealing with anyone else. She made her way out to her car—an old Porsche 911 she and Quinn were restoring together. Once her groceries were safely stowed, she got in the car and sat for a few long moments. Her hands were shaking as she reached down to start the engine. It never seemed to get any easier, dealing with people and crowds, and Memphis wondered if it ever would.

"Of course it will get better," Kieran informed her a little while later in their house, even as she reached out to smooth Memphis' hair back off her forehead. "The woman sounds like she startled you, and if she was being grabby, no one likes that."

Memphis inhaled deeply through her nose, blowing it out slowly, even as she nodded. "You're right, I know you're right."

"So maybe now isn't the time to tell you that BJ called while you were out." Memphis immediately looked tense again. "You haven't told him yet, have you?"

Pressing her lips together looking circumspect, Memphis shook her head, "I was hoping he wouldn't get back around to it, since I've been doing so much soundtrack work for Legend's movies. Do you think that's what he's calling about? Did he say something?"

"He asked me if you've been writing songs…"

Memphis winced, "Yeah, that's definitely not good."

"Well, maybe you could do an album, but not tour," Kieran offered.

"Nah, BJ thinks it's imperative to tour to support an album."

"Oh." Kieran's face fell. She knew that Memphis had enjoyed making the album she'd done, but that the touring, and too many fans grabbing at her had made her really uncomfortable.

"I'm just going to have to tell him once and for all," Memphis said, knowing telling BJ Sparks that she no longer wanted to record her own music was going to irritate him no end. It wasn't a conversation she was looking forward to, but she knew it needed to happen. She sighed to herself, then pointedly found something else to do that day.

London, England

"She's better," Remi told BJ over the phone.

"Good!" BJ responded happily, sounding immensely relieved. "How are the rest of you?"

"We are fine," Remi commented, as she watched Wynter make herself coffee. "It's all about herd immunity, right?"

BJ growled, rolling his eyes on his end. It was the latest push to come out of the English government that if allowed to run rampant through the country, people would become immune to the virus. Many scientists had already disavowed the concept, stating it would likely kill many people and overwhelm medical facilities.

"Do you think she'll be up for some press next week?"

Remi grimaced but knew that Wynter was anxious to get out the word that she was fine. The doctors still believed that she'd simply been exhausted and wasn't a victim of the virus.

"I am sure she'd like to do that," Remi stated, non-committal. Reaching up she rubbed her eyes wearily. She had a killer headache that morning; it had taken a lot of stretching and even the rarely taken medication to get it down to a manageable level.

"Good, okay, well, we'll get that set then." BJ nodded at his end, ignoring the fact that Remi hadn't endorsed the idea. "In the meantime, just do your best to stay away from people there."

"Got it."

February 20, 2019

"It's everywhere!" Finely exclaimed as she showered.

"Meaning what?" Kai asked, as she sat on the bathroom counter getting her daily updates from her fiancée.

"This crazy Coronavirus thing!" Finley's voice was muted by the water as she washed her face and hair thoroughly. "We've got sixteen cases in California!"

"Doesn't sound like much…" Kai reasoned.

The shower door was snatched open and an angry woman with shampoo running down her face gave her a narrowed look. "The death toll from this virus is currently higher than the SARS outbreak in 2002! This shit is series Kai!"

Kai took a deep breath in through her nose, pressing her lips together as she nodded, "Okay, babe, I understand."

"Do you?"

Kai spread her hands plaintively, "What can I do?"

Finley turned off the shower and Kai handed her a large bath sheet. When Finley emerged from the shower, she gave Kai a stern look.

"I just want you to be careful, please," she said, leaning her wet head against Kai's shoulder, "I know I sound like a crazy person but that moron in the White House isn't taking this seriously at all, and people are listening to him. It terrifies me."

"So it's really that bad?" Kai's tone was sincere.

Finley drew in a deep breath, expelling it as she nodded vehemently. "It's bad. What they aren't telling people is that the number of cases doubled last week. It's moving fast and it's killing people. And it's already here, it will just get worse."

Kai hugged Finley to her, knowing that it was all she could do to help. Things got worse the next day. Walking into the kitchen the next morning, she noted Finley was on the phone and looking worried.

"Wait, wait, how?" Finely queried, Wynter was talking so fast.

"They think she got it from me!" Wynter exclaimed, gripping the phone tighter.

"I thought they said it was exhaustion…" Finley began shaking her head even as her voice trailed off, they were still learning so much about the virus. "Okay, so what's going on right now?" To bring Kai into the conversation, she put the call on speaker.

"Remi was getting headaches, which is weird for her," Wynter related, "but night before last she spiked a fever, and it wouldn't go away." Finley nodded on her end, glancing at Kai, who looked worried now too. "So the advice nurse we talked to said we should bring her in."

"Okay, that's when they did the test?"

"Right," Wynter answered, sounding like she was near tears, "and now they want to keep her here, but she doesn't want to stay. What do I do?" Wynter cried, sounding panicked.

"Okay, I need you to calm down." Finley told her, her tone soothing. "Why did they say they want to keep her?"

"They didn't really, the just said they're admitting her, and Remi is arguing with them."

"Okay, any chance I can talk to someone there? Is the doctor that saw her around?"

Kai nodded, her eyes connecting with Finley's. Remi and Kai shared the bond of having been deployed together. While deployed Remi had been hurt, it had been Kai who'd helped dig her out after Kai's K-9 had located her. Remi felt that she owed Kai her life for that, but Kai never felt that way. Regardless, Kai was worried for her friend right now, having heard from her wife the seriousness of the virus.

There was rustling as Wynter held the phone to her chest trying to get someone's attention. It took a few minutes, but finally a voice came on the line.

"This is Dr. Tolliver, to whom am I speaking?" the woman's tone was heavily accented in clipped English, and she sounded very officious.

"Good afternoon, this is Dr. Finley Taylor. I'm an emergency surgeon at Cedars Sinai in Los Angeles, California, I'm also a friend of Remington LaRoché. Can I please ask why you are admitting her?"

"Officially, I shouldn't be sharing her medical information with you, but since her wife gave permission, I shall. Ms. LaRoché has been diagnosed with COVID-19 and is therefore being quarantined here at the Royal London Hospital."

"Is she in need of ICU care?" Finley asked, her tone matching that of the bureaucratic Dr. Tolliver.

"Not at this time, but—"

"Then there's no need to keep her in the hospital," Finley surmised.

"She's an American!" the doctor exclaimed. "We cannot have her infecting our citizens in a public housing situation."

"She and her wife are in a flat, not in a hotel," Finley informed the doctor.

"I, well, I was not aware of that."

"Did you ask?" Finley dead panned.

"I did not," The woman acceded. "I will see to it Ms. LaRoché is released with instructions."

"Thank you! Can I please speak with her wife again?"

"Yes ma'am." The doctor handed the phone back to Wynter with a nod of apology.

"Wow!" Wynter exclaimed. "That was easy."

"Well, the hospital assumed that you two were tourists, and therefore needed to be kept away from the general population," Finley practically growled, annoyed by the attitude of the hospital and by association the doctor. "But you have to promise me to monitor Remi's breathing. If it starts getting hard for her to breathe, you need to make sure you get her right back to the hospital, okay? Don't wait. In fact, see if you can get someone to tell you where you can pick up a pulse oximeter. They usually sell them at drug stores. If she gets below ninety-two per cent I want you headed back to the hospital right away, okay?"

"Okay, I saw a pharmacy out on Whitechapel Road, right across the street from the hospital, I'll have the car stop there one our way back to the flat."

"She'll need to quarantine, Wynter," Finley told their friend, "is that doable in that flat?"

"Yes." Wynter nodded on her end. "BJ actually managed to get us a three-bedroom flat, so there's a room right next to one of the bathrooms we can be in."

"Wynter…" Finley began.

"Don't tell me I can't be with her, Fin! I won't do that!" Wynter exclaimed, startling one of the people sitting near her at the hospital. "She didn't leave me when I was sick," she reasoned in a quieter voice.

"You guys didn't know you had the virus then," Finley told her.

"But doesn't that mean I'm immune now? I mean, isn't that the whole herd immunity bullshit they're selling over here?" Wynter noted the sharp look she got from one of the nurses who'd just walked by.

"You said it, Wyn, it's bullshit. We don't know if having the virus already keeps you from getting it again, and it could hit you worse this time. Remi wouldn't want that."

On her end of the line, Wynter curled up her lips in frustration, determined to take care of Remi and not willing to be talked out of it. Finley could sense it on her end of the call.

"Okay," Finley sighed, knowing she wasn't going to win, "but promise me you'll wear a mask and try to keep your distance."

"I'll try," Wynter replied. "Thanks again, Fin, I really appreciate your help. You all stay safe back home!"

"We will, give Remi our love!"

***

"What's wrong?" Kieran asked when she walked into hers and Memphis' bedroom that afternoon. Memphis was lying in bed with a washcloth on her face.

"Headache," Memphis mumbled.

"Was Sarah that off key?" Kieran grinned. Memphis had previously complained about Sarah Kinney, a new singer that BJ was trying out.

"Mmm," Memphis grunted non-committally, "I think my allergies are hating this spring weather we're having."

33

"Oh," Kieran moved to the bed, sitting down next to Memphis and lifting the washcloth, "did you take anything for it?"

Memphis wrinkled up her nose, "Fin said I should use that sinus rinse thing."

"And have you?" Kieran prompted.

"I don't like it," Memphis pouted, "it gives me that just-jumped-into-the-pool-without-holding-my-nose feeling."

Kieran chuckled softly. "Yes, but if Finley told you to do it, she knows best, right?"

"Just because she's a doctor, doesn't mean she knows everything," Memphis commented stubbornly.

"You're right," Kieran nodded, "she doesn't know anything about DJing or sound engineering."

Memphis narrowed her blue eyes at her wife. "You're being a smart ass."

"And you're being..." Kieran sing-songed.

"A dumb ass," Memphis sighed.

"Indeed," Kieran smiled, "I'll start the shower for you, so you can get some steam assistance. I'll even get your sinus rinse mixed up for you."

"So kind," Memphis said, making a face at her wife, then plopped the washcloth back on her face.

Kieran laughed, getting up to start the shower. Living with Memphis was sometimes like living with a petulant child, other times like living with a hyper-focused musician, and still other times like living with shut in. Memphis would often become a bit fearful of being out in the public and would put off doing small tasks to avoid it. It was no wonder with what the young woman had been through in her life, she was always worried about running into someone else from the cult she'd escaped from. She lived in a general state of fear at times, and it broke Kieran's heart a little every time. It was worse at this point in time, because Memphis' most staunch protectors, Remi and Quinn, were on tour with their wives.

Kieran started the shower and let the steam build up in the bathroom. Then she added the salt to the sinus since bottle Finley had given Memphis for her allergies. Finley had told Memphis that it was a better way to handle her allergy issues, since medications tended to have a strong effect on her. She'd been right, and it did tend the help Memphis much more than medication did. It didn't make her like it anymore, however.

Later that evening, Finley called to tell them about Remi being diagnosed with Coronavirus.

"Is she going to be okay?" Memphis asked, gripping the phone tightly.

"Wynter is going to take care of her, and I've told her what to watch out for," Finley stated, knowing full well she wasn't answering the question that Memphis had asked.

"Fin…" Memphis began, tears forming in her eyes as she did.

"I'm sorry, Memphis," Finley sighed, knowing she wasn't helping matters at that point, but refusing to lie to the younger woman. "I really am. You know you can call Wynter for updates."

"I understand." Memphis nodded, her tone curt, but knowing that she had no right to demand that Finley tell her everything would be okay. "You be safe."

"I'm trying the best that I can."

"Good, we need you here." It was Memphis' way of apologizing. "Hug Kai for me."

"Will do. You be safe out there too."

"Will do." Memphis echoed.

Memphis was exceptionally quiet that night. She did, however, wake up at 2 in the morning to call Wynter in London to ask how Remi was doing.

"She's resting," Wynter told her, "I promise to take really good care of her."

"But you're okay, right? And Xandy and Quinn?"

"We're fine!" Quinn called, as Wynter turned her phone to where Xandy and Quinn sat drinking coffee at the table in the dining room.

"See?" Wynter said, smiling as she pointed the camera back at her. "You sound stuffy though."

"Yeah, my allergies are going crazy here. We're in kind of an early spring, it's like seventy-five degrees outside and everything is blooming!"

"Do what Fin told ya to do!" Quinn called out.

"I am!" Memphis retorted.

It was a short call, but it made Memphis feel better and she was able to finally get some sleep that night.

Chapter 2

38 Cases/2 Deaths in California
88,394 Cases Worldwide/3,051 Deaths

March 1, 2020

"So, what are our options?" Midnight asked the woman sitting across from her.

"We have to start thinking in terms of managing the spread," Marilyn Point, the head of the Department of Public Health, told her. Her dark brown eyes reflected the worry that she'd been harboring since the first time she'd heard about Coronavirus.

"What's that going to look like?" Midnight asked, glancing at her Lieutenant Governor, Shea Gorman.

Shea nodded, "Exactly, how can we do that? We can't exactly close the State off."

Marilyn chewed on the inside of her cheek. "That's actually not far off of what I'm suggesting."

Midnight blinked a couple of times. "Are you serious?"

Marilyn noted that the usually unflappable Governor currently looked fairly alarmed.

"I don't think we're there yet," Marilyn assured, putting a comforting hand on Midnight's arm, "but we need to start looking at easing group gatherings. One area is in schools."

"Schools?" Shea repeated, "What level?"

"All of them," Midnight answered, having started thinking of that the moment Marilyn had said it. Marilyn nodded, once again astounded at how quickly Midnight Chevalier caught up and seized on a concept. "We need to start talking to the school districts, we need less places for this stuff to spread." She looked at Marilyn again. "What else?"

Marilyn pursed her lips, drawing in a deep breath and blowing it out slowly, worried about her next statement. "We need to think about declaring a State of Emergency. As you've probably seen, a lot of the local counties have done it, but we need to do it at the State level."

Shea was on her phone the moment the words "State of Emergency" were out of Marilyn's mouth. "Okay, so that means being able to secure federal funds to help with this, it also makes all of the State's resources available for moving forward."

Marilyn was nodding as Shea spoke.

"Let's start heading in that direction then." Midnight looked resolved as she stood up. There was a lot to think about and discuss; she knew she needed to start pulling in her heads of State. Things were getting serious.

***

"Where are you now?" Parker asked, having lost track of Talon's movements. "I can't keep up with your schedule!".

"We're in Sri Lanka. The minute we got here they told us we had to quarantine, since we were in South Korea last," Talon said.

38

Parker blew out her breath loudly. "So where are you stuck then?"

Talon smiled. "Oh trust me, I'm not stuck… You should see this place! The resort is called Uga Chena Huts, and they are absolutely beautiful!"

"Huts?" Parker replied, imagining some ramshackle building with no running water.

"Oh, it's not like it sounds," Talon told her, "I'm sitting on my personal patio, and it's pointed right at the ocean. My hut has its own pool! I'm definitely not suffering right now."

"As long as you're safe," Parker said, having heard from others that the virus was spreading rapidly, and it sounded like it was only going to get worse.

"I am," Talon assured, feeling a warm glow that Parker was worried about her. "How is everything there?"

"Kim is freaking out about this COVID thing, Finley is making sure everyone is wearing masks and doing that stay away from each other thing."

"It is bad there?"

"Not too bad, I think last time Fin updated everyone she said it was like thirty-something cases in California, but it's sounding pretty scary."

"Well, you make sure you're being safe."

"Doing what I can, wearing a mask, trying to stay away from people. Not that people are cooperating too much right now." Parker rolled her eyes Heavenward. "Everyone is listening to the Twitler who said it's basically the flu."

"Yeah, I heard about that. He's definitely not helping the situation." Talon had seen enough American news to see that the President of the United States was calling the virus a hoax and saying it would just go away when it got warm. "I can only imagine how pissed off Finley is about it."

"Oh trust me, she's plenty pissed. Did you hear about Wynter and Remi having the virus?"

"Oh shit! No!" Talon came halfway out of her chair in surprise. "Are they okay?"

"Wynter's better, but they didn't know she had it, so Remi was taking care of her and now Remi has it."

"Yikes, well, if you talk to either of them send my love."

"Ten-four," Parker confirmed while trying to stifle a yawn. "Sorry babe."

"I know, it's getting late there," Talon sighed, glancing at her watch which was still set to LA time. Even though it was twelve thirty in the afternoon in Sri Lanka, it was eleven at night in Los Angeles. "I love you, be safe!"

"Love you." Parker smiled.

"Give Kim and Ginny hugs from me."

"Absolutely."

After hanging up, Talon sat watching the waves roll in and thought about home. She was doing her best not to worry, but she knew she needed to be where Parker and the girls were. It felt completely wrong to be here surrounded by palm trees and sand, with room service and her every need met. It was one of those moments in her life where she felt the weight of so-called stardom isolating her. She received a level of preference that we beyond what most people ever felt. Narrowing her eyes, she started thinking about what she could do right now to help. Her next call was to Finley.

"I couldn't tell you what Sri Lanka needs, Tal, but I can tell you what's happening here. People are crazy buying stuff! Shelves are empty! You can't get meat, you can't get bread, you can't get pasta, rice or beans!"

Talon nodded. "I imagine that'll be worse on a small island like this."

"If it hasn't happened already. News of this stuff is spreading fast."

"So what can I do to help the medical community? Anything?" Talon queried next.

"PPE, personal protective equipment! We're running out of gloves, masks, gowns, even crazy shit like hand sanitizer!"

"I should be able to search on Google for that, right?"

"Probably." Fin nodded at her end.

"I'll send some for Cedars too, who should I send it to care of? You?"

"That would be so amazing Tal! Thank you! You have no idea…" Finley's voice trailed off as she shook her head. "We just weren't prepared for this. There are stores of PPE somewhere with the feds, but the damned administration won't bother to release it. Ten bucks says the President is selling it off."

"Knowing the level of shit this guy is capable of, I wouldn't doubt it for a second," Talon agreed.

"Oh, and where to send it—send it to Sharon Bettega, she's our supply manager. She'll be better able to distribute it."

"You got it! Stay safe over there, please!"

"Doing my best. There's only been two deaths in California so far, but the cases are climbing. You stay safe there too, Tal."

"Isolated in a super hut on the beach at this point." Talon chuckled.

"Rough gig," Finley murmured, smiling as she did.

Three days later, Talon had acquired a respectable amount of PPE, some of which she sent to Cedars Sinai in Los Angeles, and the rest she donated to the local hospitals in Sri Lanka. She also made a point of acquiring rice, lentils and various other ingredients for popular Sri Lankan dishes in large quantities and had them delivered to various food banks on the island. She figured it was the least she could do for the people of Sri Lanka. The donations were made anonymously, Talon was never one to want credit for things.

***

"How long has it been?" the nurse asked, looking up from her clipboard.

"Um, like a week?" Memphis said, her voice displaying how stuffed up her sinuses were.

The nurse nodded, writing down the information. "The doctor should be in in a few minutes," she said, then exited the room.

"This is stupid," Memphis told Kieran.

"It's not stupid, you probably have an infection and just need more than what we've been doing."

"I didn't mean being here," Memphis said, leaning her head against the wall. She liked the feel of the cool walls, her head felt like it was going to split in half at that point. "I mean not seeing Finley."

"Finley is so busy right now, love, I don't want to bother her with this," Kieran reasoned.

Memphis screwed up her lips in a grimace. "I know, you're right. Geeze, my frigging teeth hurt! I feel like my nose is like ten times its normal size!"

She'd been in a lot of pain over the last couple of days and Kieran had finally practically dragged her out of the house to go to the doctor. Memphis still didn't trust doctors, except for Finley. Since her time with the cult, where the doctors essentially said whatever "the prophet" wanted them to say to young girls to encourage them to be "good proper" girls, Memphis avoided the medical profession unless absolutely necessary. Kieran had told her this was one of those times.

A half an hour later they left the doctor's office with a prescription for antibiotics. The doctor had also given Memphis a shot of Toradol, an anti-inflammatory that helped take away some of the pain in her head. She slept well for the first time in days that night.

March 3, 2020

"What did the doctor say?" Legend asked. Even as she got into her car to head home, it was one o'clock in the morning in Los Angeles: it had been a long night.

"I didn't go," Riley replied listlessly.

"You promised." Legend sighed, even as she started up her Barracuda with a loud rumble.

"Where are you?" Riley queried, having just heard Legend's car. "Are you just leaving the studio?"

"Don't try to change the subject," Legend admonished, even as she grimaced.

"You don't change the subject, you're supposed to be trying not to overdo it!"

"Well, you're not here to keep me distracted," Legend grinned, her eyes sparkling mischievously.

"Don't give me that, Ustura Leora Azaria!" Riley snapped.

"Doh!" Legend exclaimed. "Pulling out the full-on Hebrew, huh? Low blow."

"You promised me you wouldn't over obsess on this picture," Riley reminded her.

"And you promised me you'd go to the doctor to make sure you're not sick with that Corona shit," Legend countered.

Riley sighed at her end of the line. "I know."

"But?" Legend prompted.

"But everything is so frigging chaotic here, I just don't have the energy to deal with it."

"So production is completely shut?"

"At this point, yeah," Riley said, "I mean they only have like 300 or so cases, but the government is freaking out."

"Yeah, things are going crazy here too, everything is selling out. The shelves are empty here."

"Wow, really?" Riley asked, shocked. "I didn't figure America would freak out, we always have so much of everything."

"Not right now." Legend shook her head as she turned down Sunset. The streets were surprisingly and eerily quiet. "You can't find meat, and now the big thing seems to be frigging toilet paper."

"Seriously?" Riley deadpanned.

"Yeah, it's sold out everywhere! It's crazy!"

"Does the virus cause major diarrhea or something?"

"No!" Legend laughed. "I have no idea why people are hoarding this shit like crazy. Between that, hand sanitizer and Lysol wipes, people are stockpiling the stuff and reselling it for super profit. I'm beginning to think we should have bought stock in Charmin!"

Riley laughed at her end. She was laying in her hotel bed, where she'd been for what seemed like days. She felt really melancholy at that point; without the movie work to keep her busy, she was missing home. In fact, she didn't think she'd ever missed Legend more. At home they had such a nice routine. Even when Legend was working on a movie, as long as she was in town they always had breakfast together, talking about the day's plans or current events. It was a time when they could simply focus on each other and nothing else. For Riley, having someone who cared about her as a person, not as an object, "a star", or meal ticket was something she'd never had before, and she prized it above everything else. Legend was everything she never realized she'd needed, and Riley missed that closeness.

"Where'd you go, babe?" Legend asked softly.

Riley smiled at the sound; her wife always noticed when she grew quiet—yet another difference. "I'm just missing home today."

"I miss you too, Ri," Legend told her, "maybe you should just come home."

"If things don't open back up, I might," Riley said, feeling her spirits lift a bit with the possibility. "We'll see how things look next week. Maybe they'll get a handle on things. Figure out how to operate a movie set safely, or something."

"Or something," Legend echoed with a laugh.

"I love you," Riley told her sincerely.

"And I love you," Legend replied with equal earnestness.

March 4, 2020

"This isn't headed in a good direction babe," Wynter told Remi as she looked at the reading for her oxygen levels. "I need to get you back to the hospital."

Remi nodded, looking exhausted. Her breathing had become more and more labored, and Wynter didn't want to wait anymore. Getting up from the chair she'd been sitting in, she stuck her head out the bedroom door.

"Quinn!" she called, the Irishwoman responded immediately, even though it was the middle of the night.

"What's up?" Quinn asked, already on high alert as she pulled her shirt down over her job bra. She'd been sleeping but had made a point in the last day or two of sleeping in her bra and sweats with socks in on case she was needed.

"We need to get her downstairs, her oxygen levels are dropping too fast."

"Do you want to call an ambulance?" Quinn pulled out her phone even as she asked.

"I'd rather we take her, I've been hearing the response times for ambulances are delayed. I think we can get her there faster."

"Call downstairs, have them grab a car, I'll drive," Quinn told her, "I'm gonna let Xan know and throw on some shoes, then I'll be back to help you with her."

"Okay," Wynter said, doing her best not to lose her mind. Remi needed her right now, she couldn't lose it, not yet.

Picking up her phone, she called down to the building concierge, thanking the gods that BJ had put them in a building with a service.

The young man, who'd already been on alert for any emergency to do with Remington LaRoché, told her it would be waiting out front. He asked if she needed assistance, she told him that she didn't.

Ten minutes later, she and Quinn got Remi into the backseat of the car. Another ten minutes and they were at the Emergency Room where chaos reigned. There were people everywhere, and three ambulances parked in the bay. Not that that deterred Quinn.

"Stay here," Quinn told Wynter, then got out of the car and strode toward the entrance.

Wynter got into the back seat with Remi and did her best to comfort her wife. Remi was very obviously out of it, as if she was only concentrating on breathing.

"Quinn will get you in there, don't worry."

"Wyn…" Remi replied, her voice soft and halting between gasping breaths, "if some…thing…"

"Stop," Wynter told her, tears in her eyes instantly as she knew what Remi was going to say. Something along the lines of if something were to happen, she loved Wynter and was ready to go if it was her time. "You are going to be fine."

Remi shook her head but didn't try to tell Wynter again. She knew that things would go the way they were meant to go. If the universe was ready to take her, then that's what would happen. It wasn't that she wasn't scared—having been struggling to breathe for the last day was terrifying—but she also knew that things were going haywire in the world, and that railing against Fate would do her no good.

A minute later, two men came out with a wheelchair and immediately helped Remi from the vehicle. Quinn and Wynter were told they'd have to wait in the waiting room to talk to the doctor.

"We'll wait out here in the car," Quinn told one of the men, "make sure the doctors know to call us out here." The men nodded and walked away with Remi.

"I didn't even get a chance to…" Wynter murmured, but stopped herself, even as Quinn shook her head.

"It wasn't goodbye," Quinn told her firmly. Wynter just nodded, doing her best not to cry. Quinn put her arm around Wynter's shoulders, hugging her close. "She'll be okay, Remi is tough as they come."

It was another two hours until the doctor walked out to their car, knocking on the window. Wynter climbed out the car and Quinn did the same, walking around to stand next to Wynter.

"Are you Ms. LaRoché's family?" the doctor with the clipped English accent asked.

"I'm her wife." Wynter nodded.

The man blinked a couple of times, as if he couldn't understand what she just said, then finally nodded. "Your wife is very sick."

Wynter nodded. "Can you help her?"

"We want to put her on a ventilator right away, for that we will need to put her in a medically induced coma. We will need your permission."

Wynter stared back at the man open mouthed, as he held up a clipboard with a form attached to it. Her brain was trying to catch up with what he had just said. "Coma?" she repeated.

"Yes ma'am," the doctor nodded, pushing the form at her again.

"Wait, I…" Wynter began, shaking her head, putting her hand out to ward off the clipboard. "I need to… I have to call…"

"Ma'am this needs to be done right away," the doctor insisted.

"Just hold on!" Quinn snapped at the man, even as she pulled out her phone and dialed Finley's number. Thankfully, Finley answered on the second ring. "Fin, it's me, we got a doctor here wanting to put Remi in a damned coma, can you talk to him?"

"I, uh, sure," Finley stammered.

Quinn promptly handed the doctor the phone, her eyes narrowed. "She's a doctor too."

"Hello?" the Englishman queried.

"Hi, this is Dr. Finley Taylor, Cedars Sinai. I'm sorry for my Irish friend's manner, but they are very worried about your patient and need reassurance," Finley started.

The conversation between the two doctors took a few long minutes, but then he handed the phone to Wynter. "She says she needs to speak with you."

Wynter took the phone with shaking hands. "Y-yes?"

"Wynter, you need to sign the form, now," Finley instructed, "then I'll explain what's happening." Wynter did as instructed, and the doctor took it and strode back into the hospital. "Did you sign it?"

"Yes," Wynter told her.

"Okay, what they are doing is necessary Wynter," Finley told her gently.

"What does it mean? Coma sounds scary."

"They are going to sedate Remi, and then put a breathing tube down her throat, it's attached to a machine that will push oxygen into her lungs. Then they're going to give her medication through an IV that will basically make her go to sleep. The ventilator does the work of oxygenating her blood, so her body doesn't have to keep straining to do it. That lets her body focus on fighting the virus. The coma will keep her calm, not making her feel the discomfort of the breathing tube. Okay? It's for the very best, we're doing that here with patients too."

"You are?" Wynter asked.

"Yes," Finley said, praying Wynter wouldn't ask if it was working or not, because at that point it wasn't truly working well, but she'd told Wynter the truth. It was likely the best chance Remi had.

"Okay," Wynter nodded at her end. "Thank you, Finley."

"The doctor said he'd come back and get you to so you can talk to Remi before they put her under, it'll be through glass and on a cell phone, but at least you'll get to tell her you love her and that you'll see her soon."

Ten minutes later, Wynter was led to the outside of a room where Remington lay in a bed. Wynter had her phone, and Remi was handed one of the nurse's. They were told to keep the conversation short.

"Love you," Remi said immediately.

"I love you," Wynter told her, "I'll be right here when you wake up, okay? You just get in there and kick this virus's ass."

"Wi mal," Remington breathed, saying 'yes ma'am' in Creole.

Their eyes connected as the nurse in the room administered the sedative. Wynter kept her eyes on Remi the entire time until Remi's hazel eyes closed.

"We will take good care of your love, miss," The dark-haired nurse, whose name badge read Cynthia, told her. Wynter saw the woman's eyes crinkle at the corner as she smiled behind her mask. "I'm a big fan of your love story."

Wynter sighed, she hoped that meant this woman would take extra good care of Remi. "Thank you so much, for everything," Wynter told the nurse. She then pulled a note card out of her jacket pocket, writing her cell phone number on it and handed it to Cynthia. "Will you call me night or day if there's any change?" she pleaded.

"Of course." Cynthia nodded, a mist of tears gathering in her warm brown eyes.

A half an hour later, she and Quinn arrived back at the flat. Wynter went immediately into the original bedroom she and Remi had been sharing. She closed the door softly and crawled into bed fully clothed, kicking off her tennis shoes and pulled the covers up over her. Finally, she gave in to the urge to cry.

Quinn walked into kitchen, where Xandy stood making coffee. Quinn immediately hugged her wife, feeling grateful they'd been healthy thus far but at the same time feeling awful that her friend was so sick.

"What happened?" Xandy asked softly.

"They put Remi in a coma and on a ventilator."

"Oh lord…" Xandy breathed. Quinn grimaced and hugged Xandy tighter. "Is she going to get better?"

"No one knows, Fin said it's for the best, but I don't think she told us everything either."

Xandy pressed her lips together in a frown, nodding her head. The idea that Remi, who Xandy considered one of the strongest and healthiest among them, could die from this terrible virus was simply terrifying.

"I gotta call BJ," Quinn told Xandy.

Minutes later BJ answered his cell phone, Quinn relayed the information.

"Son of a bitch…" BJ gasped in shock. He'd known that Remi was sick, but he, like everyone else, had assumed she'd bounce right back. "What do you need? Anything? What can I do?"

Quinn shook her head at her end, sighing as she did. "Nothing, man, the house is great, it just sucks being here right now."

"I know I can count on you to take care of our girls," BJ said, "but if anything comes up, or you need anything, I don't care what it is. You call me. Okay?"

"Got it," Quinn acknowledges. "How are things there? You all doing okay?"

"Yeah, we're good, just trying to keep things going. Midnight declared a State of Emergency last night, so everyone is flipping out a bit."

"We saw that on the news. This is some crazy times we're livin' in."

"Too right," BJ agreed whole-heartedly.

***

Memphis was doing her best to concentrate on the singer in the booth, but she just couldn't focus. She'd been working almost non-stop in the last three days since the antibiotics had helped to calm her sinuses. Not having a headache had made it much easier to handle having headphones on in the sound booth. She'd been feeling better ever since they'd given her the shot of Toradol, and she'd gone back to work with a vengeance.

"What am I missing?" the singer queried, her voice strident. She easily sensed that the sound engineer wasn't paying attention.

"What?" Memphis queried, shivering as she pulled her hoodie closer around her ears.

"Are you even here?" the middle-aged singer queried sharply.

"I'm sorry, Tam, I'm not having a good day right now," Memphis apologized.

"Well, I don't have time for this right now." Tammy rolled her over-large eyes, fluffing out her eighties hair.

"I'm sorry, can we just call it today? I'll work with you again next week, okay?"

Tammy huffed but didn't dare get snottier with Memphis Lassiter: this was probably her last chance to get back into the music business. The last thing she wanted to do was piss off BJ's favorite.

"Fine," Tammy finally blurted out, hanging her headphones up.

"Thank you," Memphis spoke into the mic, knowing she was pissing the has-been off but not really caring.

An hour later she was home and sitting in front of the gas fireplace, wearing a blanket around her, along with sweatpants a hoodie and thick socks. She was sipping tea from a huge mug. Kieran found her there two hours later.

"What's wrong?" Kieran asked, noting the way that Memphis was bundled up.

"I can't get warm." Memphis' teeth chattered as she spoke.

"Have you tried a nice hot shower?" Kieran asked.

"No, maybe I should."

"Let me get the bathroom warmed up first," Kieran offered.

A little while later, Kieran had the space heater running in the bathroom. She'd turned the shower on, and let it steam up and warm up the room. She helped Memphis undress and got her into the shower, making sure she was comfortable.

"I'll be right outside," she told Memphis.

In their bedroom, Kieran got on the phone to call Finley. She was worried that Memphis had somehow contracted the virus that was going around.

"I'm sorry honey, she's in the middle of a surgery," Jacks told the young English girl, "I'll give her a message to call you, okay?"

"Yes please, tell her it's Memphis, she's sick," Kieran told the older nurse that was Finley's friend.

"You got it, sweetie," Jacks said, snapping her gum as she glanced up at the clock to write the time on the message.

They didn't hear from Finley until the middle of the night. Finley said that Memphis definitely needed to get a test.

"Where can we go?" Kieran asked.

"At this point, with the Governor declaring a State of Emergency, everything is going crazy." Finley said, shaking her head, "I don't want you two anywhere near here. If you think she doesn't have it, she could before she gets out of the ER. I'll see if I can get my hands on a test and come do it, okay? Just try to keep her warm and make sure she stays hydrated."

"Okay," Kieran nodded, looking over at Memphis who was huddled under multiple blankets on the bed.

"Do not let her leave the house, Kier, okay? No work, no-where." Finley's tone was stern.

"I won't," Kieran told her, "I'll take the day off tomorrow, so I can be here with her."

"Good." Finley nodded.

March 5, 2020

The next day they got the word about Remi from Quinn.

"That's really bad, isn't it?" Memphis asked, gripping the phone tightly as she did her best to keep from freaking completely out.

At her end, Quinn grimaced, having known that this would be hard on Memphis. "It's not great, Mem, but it's supposed to help her."

"How?" Memphis asked softly.

"She has to be on a ventilator and putting her out means she won't be freaking out trying to deal with it. It's better for her."

Memphis shook her head on her end of the line, her mind filling with images of Remi being in a hospital bed with tubes and a mask and struggling to breathe. It broke her heart into a million pieces.

That night, Memphis laid in bed and cried while Kieran held her. Kieran felt horrible that there was really nothing she could do or say to help Memphis handle this latest set of bad news. The idea that Memphis too might have this horrible virus terrified Kieran. She did her best not to show that fear to Memphis, wanting only to support her during this awful time in their lives.

March 6, 2020

It took Finley two days to get her hands on and administer a test. She wore full PPE, including face mask, shield, goggles, gloves and a gown that she took out of the package before she let Kieran even open the front door.

"Okay, Mem, this is going to suck," she told Memphis, "this test is kind of jarring, I'm just warning you."

Memphis looked immediately wary. "What does that mean? What do you have to do?"

Finley took a long skinny stick-looking object out of a plastic tube. "Okay, this is a swab that I'm going to have to put up your nose and twirl around for like ten seconds, and then I have to do the other nostril."

Memphis shrugged. "Both?"

"Yeah, both."

"Why?"

"We have to collect enough mucus at the back of your sinuses to test it."

"That doesn't sound bad."

Finley's lips tugged down in a grimace. "I've had more than one, trust me it's not a comfortable feeling, but we need to know if you've got this damned virus, okay?"

Memphis inhaled deeply, nodding as she blew her breath out. "Got it."

"Okay, Kieran, sit her down in that chair there." Finley directed them to a high-backed chair in the living room. "Now Memphis, put your head back against that headrest. Don't move when I put this in, no matter how much you want to."

"No moving, got it," Memphis repeated.

Finley moved in to use the swab. Memphis instantly knew what Finley had been talking about. It felt like a tiny little bee was on the end of the stick and it was stinging her over and over as Finley swirled the swab in her first nostril.

"Holy crap, holy crap!" Memphis chanted as she did her best not to squirm away from the hateful swab.

57

"I know, I'm sorry..." Finley sympathized as she pulled the swab out.

"You have to do that again?" Memphis complained.

"Yep," Finley nodded. "You ready?"

"Not really, no," Memphis muttered, her blue eyes wide.

Finley pressed her lips together under her mask, even when she was sick, Memphis was so endearingly cute. She just loved this girl and she really hoped she didn't have COVID.

"I should have the results in a few days. In the meantime, stay home, do not go anywhere," Finley cautioned Memphis again. Kieran walked Finley out to her car. As she took off the gown and gloves Finley gave Kieran a serious look. "You really shouldn't be around her right now, you know that right?"

Kieran stared back at her with wide eyes. "But...she needs me..."

"I know," Finley nodded, sighing, she'd heard it so many times already, "but the fact is that it's very contagious and she can give it to you. If I could have gotten my hands on a second test, I would have given you one too."

"What difference does it make?" Kieran said, shrugging. "If I get it, I'll deal with it, but I'm not abandoning Memphis."

Finley shook her head. "This is nasty stuff, Kier, it really is."

"We've been through worse."

Finley didn't have an answer for that.

March 7, 2020

Three days later, things were much worse. Memphis could barely get out of bed without breathing heavily. She wasn't eating, saying that she felt sick to her stomach. By the weekend, Kieran was terribly worried; that was when she got a call from Finley telling her that Memphis did indeed have COVID.

"How's her breathing?" Finley asked.

"She's having a hard time whenever she tries get out of bed and move around the house," Kieran told her worriedly.

Finley grimaced, shaking her head. "Okay, I'm going to send over a pulse oximeter, you'll need to put it on her finger to see what her oxygen saturation is."

"Shouldn't we just come to the hospital?" Kieran asked.

"No, hon, not right now," Finley said, "this is all getting bad, really fast and beds are filling up. Once she gets here, you can't be with her, and I know that's going to make this worse for her."

Kieran sniffed back tears, worried for Memphis, but also knowing that Finley would never steer them wrong. She refocused on the task at hand. "What do I do with this pulse thing?"

"Like I said, you'll put it on her fingertip, it will tell you how much oxygen is in her blood."

"Okay."

"You'll need to watch it, if it drops below ninety percent, I want you to call 911."

"911?" Kieran repeated sounding alarmed.

"This virus is effecting people's lungs. Oxygen saturation levels can drop quickly, and I don't want hers to drop too far before we get in her on a monitor."

"Okay," Kieran said again, feeling overwhelmed suddenly. She was going to be responsible for making sure Memphis was breathing enough. The idea of going to sleep that night suddenly became daunting. What if something happened? What if Memphis stopped breathing? What if… She squeezed her eyes shut—she couldn't think about that. Memphis was her whole world now. No one meant as much to her as Memphis did. Not even her family in England, who still didn't understand how she could be in love with a woman.

"Kieran?" Finley queried; she could hear Kieran breathing quickly. "You okay?"

"I… Yes… I just need to process this."

"It's a lot, I know." Finley felt bad for the younger woman, she knew it was terrifying to have to worry about someone you loved.

Every night the news was telling people how many cases there were in the world, over 106,000 at that point and growing every day. There were 100 cases in California already. The President of the United States was still likening it to the "flu" and talking like it wasn't a big deal at all. It was terrifying to health care workers everywhere who could see what was happening on the frontlines. If no one at the top was taking it seriously, how were the common, everyday people going to take it seriously?

That night, Finley pulled into the garage at hers and Kai's house surprised to find Kai and Dakota working in the back half of the tandem portion of the three-car garage. Getting out of her car, Finley kept her distance as she always did when getting home from the hospital these days.

"What are you doing?" Finley asked.

Kai looked up from where she and Dakota were working with PVC pipe. "Extending the back bathroom."

"For?"

"We're opening up this wall and adding a washer dryer combo, so you can come straight in here, put your scrubs in the wash and take your shower. Safer right?"

Finley felt tears sting the backs of her eyes, she'd commented to Kai over and over how worried she was that she'd spread germs to her simply by coming in without changing. It was a constant concern for her. One her fiancée had seen fit to address.

"Uh oh," Dakota murmured, when she saw tears in Finley's eyes, "the waterworks are starting."

"Just work," Kai told her with a grin. "You okay babe?" she asked Finley.

"Yes," Finley breathed nodding her head, "I just... this is so thoughtful... thank you. And thank you, Dakota."

"Don't thank me, I'm bored frigging silly right now, I was happy to have something to do!" Dakota laughed.

"She won't even let me pay her," Kai curled up her lips in disdain.

"Jaz'd kill me if I let you pay me," Dakota informed her. "Don't worry about us, we have money coming in with rentals."

"But aren't people having a hard time paying right now?" Finley asked.

"The ones that are, are doing the best they can. We're fine, Fin, I promise," Dakota assured.

Finley nodded, not wanting to insult Dakota by asking too many questions. The group had already started pulling together to make sure everyone that was in town was covered for food, supplies, and medical advice. Finley, Fadiyah and River had been fielding questions as best they could and trying to help any way they could. The richer members of the group had followed Talon's lead and started doing their best to help acquire PPE to donate to local hospitals, as well as try and track down food staples like meat, grains and fresh vegetables—both for the group and local food banks. A few of them had actually planted gardens to grow vegetables as the weather warmed up.

No one knew exactly what the future held, but as a tight knit group of friends they each pitched in where they could. Jazmine and Natalia had started doing dance classes online for their friends, so no one got out of shape, and Kai had even been convinced to do a few fitness training classes for the bois.

March 9, 2020

"Well, I guess I should've gotten out while I could," Riley told Legend.

"It's okay. How are you feeling?" Legend was more worried that she let on, but she didn't want to panic her wife.

Rome had put the city in an unprecedented lockdown. No one could enter or leave the city. There had been over 6,000 new cases of the virus reported in the last week. The government had seen no other way to attempt to slow the spread than keeping people from traveling between cities.

"I was feeling better, but today I feel trapped. I don't know, maybe I'm just getting cabin fever, and now knowing I can't go anywhere makes it feels worse."

"So what exactly is the deal there?" Legend asked, staring out at the ocean. She was sitting on the back balcony of their house.

"We're still getting details," Riley rubbed at her face, wanting to reach through the phone line and be with Legend, no matter how lousy she felt. "Sounds like we can't leave the house unless we have a good reason."

"And what's a good reason?"

"I don't really know, I guess if you have to go to work or grocery shopping."

"So you can still shop, that's good." Legend chuckled.

"Except all the good stores are closed, I already miss my farmers market."

"Well, I'm sure they don't want you guys gathering. We're in a state of emergency here."

"Yeah, but you're not stuck at home."

"Things aren't going as crazy here as it is there spread wise. California only has like 170 or so cases. You guys are in the thousands, so it's better you stay in, babe."

"I know," Riley grunted, wishing she'd just gone home the week before. She'd been worried that the minute she got back to California, production would start up again and she'd have to fly back. It was an average of a sixteen-hour flight, and then the adjustment for jet lag on top of that was grueling, definitely not something she'd relished doing twice.

March 10, 2020

It was so dark, why was it so dark? What is that buzzing, it's very annoying, femen li, turn it off! De bon, good, it's off. What is this thing in my throat? O bondye! It's a snake, I have to get it out! If I can just get a good grip...

"Cyns, get over here! She's trying to pull the tube out! She's so damned strong!"

Cynthia threw on a new gown and mask as fast as she could while her co-worker did her best to wrestle Remi's hands away from the breathing tube. It wasn't the first time they'd had a patient come partially out of the sedation. The COVID virus seemed to burn through the medication quickly at times.

"Remi, stop!" Cynthia yelled as she moved to help the other nurse. Remi's frantic movements slowed.

But it's snake? Why won't you let me get it out, it will kill me! Wait, it's… Mwen estipid, I'm so stupid, it's a hose, but why do I have a hose in my throat, this could suffocate me! Why is my right hand so heavy? I can't even lift it, ede m, help me!

"Bloody Hell, get more sedation into that IV!" Cynthia told the other nurse as Remi's movements grew frantic again, fortunately, they'd managed to get one hand into the binding on the edge of the bed, but her left was flailing madly, balled into a fist. "I do not want to get pummeled by this woman, Andrea, hurry up!"

How can I fight in the dark? I can't even see my opponent! Who fights this way? Holding my arm down so I cannot fight? Pi bon mache! Why do you cheat? Turn on the lights, let's have a real go at this!

"Blimey! Hold 'er will ya?" Andrea said, as Remi's hand swiped very close to her as she did her best to draw out the proper amount of sedation from the bottle in her hand.

"I'm tryin'! She's damned strong!" Cynthia said. "Remi! Please! It's okay! We've got you!"

Who is that? Why are you... oh... I have nothing, I cannot fight now... I feel weights on my arms...

"Oh thank the big man upstairs, she's relaxing now." Cynthia sighed.

"Just in the nick of time."

"So why did that happen?" Wynter asked of Cynthia when the nurse called that night to update her on Remi's condition.

"For some reason, the virus is interacting with some patients differently, and the sedation wears off more quickly that we expect. The doctor has adjusted her medication."

"But she's calm now?" Wynter bit her lip, doing her best not to imagine Remi in a panic with the breathing tube.

"Yes, she's calm and her oxygen levels are improving a bit." Cynthia was happy to report.

"That's good, at least. Thank you so much for calling, I really appreciate it."

"You're very welcome." Cynthia smiled at her end, Wynter Kincade was certainly nothing like what had been reported over the years. Wynter had always been reported to be high strung and a bit of a Diva.

***

"Memphis, we need to check your levels." Kieran held up the small pulse oximeter.

It was obvious to her that Memphis' breath was becoming more labored. Not surprising, however, Memphis shook her head, rubbing her cheek on the arm she had in front of her face on the pillow. She was huddled under no less than three blankets and was wearing one of her favorite hoodies with the hood up over her head. She resembled a homeless waif, and Kieran felt her heart ache with the idea of how this virus could affect the woman she loved.

"Honey, we need to monitor it," Kieran reasoned softly.

Memphis shook her head vehemently this time.

"What is happening?" Kieran queried, sensing more going on than just not wanting to be bothered at the moment.

Memphis looked back at her for a long moment, blinking repeatedly, but simply shrugged in answer. Kieran continued to stare back at her wife, trying to discern what was going on in her mind. She was stunned when tears suddenly glazed Memphis's blue eyes.

"Oh love, what is it?" Kieran begged. "Please tell me."

Memphis swallowed convulsively a few times, obviously trying to get her emotions under control. "I'm scared," she finally whispered.

"Of what?" Kieran asked, needing to know what to address.

"If that thing says I'm not breathing good, I'll have to go to the hospital… and be on a ventilator, and…" her voice trailed off as she choked back a sob. "I can't, I can't…" she chanted between sobs.

"Oh honey!" Kieran climbed onto the bed, putting her hand out to caress Memphis' cheek. "I know this is all scary and hard, but it'll be okay."

"You shouldn't be this close," Memphis told her, tears sliding from her eyes. "I don't want you to get sick."

"I'm not going to leave you in her by yourself, Memphis, I can't."

Memphis didn't respond, only rubbing her face on the arm of her hoodie. In truth, while one part of her was terrified that she'd give this to Kieran and put her life in danger, the other part of her was afraid to be alone with her own thoughts and what could happen if this virus took a turn for the worse. The very thought of dying alone in an ICU ward made Memphis feel absolutely sick. If someone like Remington LaRoché could be stuck in a medical coma and on a ventilator, Memphis reasoned in her head, what chance would she have?

"Can we please do this?" Kieran whispered finally, holding up the oximeter again.

Memphis finally stuck her finger out, looking like Kieran was about to chop it off. They both waited for the reading, feeling like it was taking forever.

"There," Kieran said when the reading came through, "it's ninety, see? We're still okay."

Memphis nodded, not looking like she felt the relief that Kieran expressed.

Later that night, Kieran was on the phone to Finley.

"I'm really worried," she told their friend, "Memphis is completely freaking out about the possibility of having to be in the hospital."

"What are her oxygen numbers looking like?" Finley glanced at her watch, it was eight thirty p.m., she was supposed to be off in a half an hour.

"Tonight it was ninety," Kieran told her.

"Damn it," Finley muttered. "I don't like that, Kieran, it's dropping steadily. How completely freaked out is she?" Finley asked, grimacing at her end.

"I'm afraid she won't go unless she's unconscious."

"She drops a few more points and she'll be there." Finley shook her head, her mind racing. "I'll be there in an hour, just keep checking that oxygen level." As soon as she hung up with Kieran, she made another call.

As promised, an hour later Finely arrived. As always, she gowned up, double masked and gloved before walking into the house.

"How are you feeling?" Finley asked Kieran first, using a handheld thermometer to check Kieran's temperature. "Any headaches, sore throat, nausea?"

"No."

"You're taking your temperature regularly?" Finley rolled out a drape on the dining room table, setting her bag on it and taking items out of it as she glanced at Kieran for her answer.

"Yes, at least three times a day like you told me."

Finley nodded, "Good. Okay, here's what I've brought." She began holding up items as she told Kieran what they were. "This is an oxygen machine," she said, putting her hand on the machine she was unboxing, "you can thank BJ Sparks for pulling a lot of strings to get ahold of this. You can't find them at this point because people are buying everything up."

Kieran's eyes widened at what Finley was saying, but she nodded as she listened to the rest of what Finley was telling her. In her head she was thanking her lucky stars that they had such wonderful friends.

"I've also talked my hospital in letting me treat Memphis as a kind of a shut in, so I've got an IV drip that I'm going to set up for her. It's an antiviral drug called Remdesivir. She's going to need a dose every day for five days."

"Will it help?" Kieran asked, praying for the right answer to come out of Finley's mouth.

Finley drew a deep breath, blowing it out slowly. "It's experimental, but it's been showing some promise, so we're going to give it a go, okay?"

Kieran nodded, tears gathering in her eyes.

"Don't cry, Kier, we'll try everything we can to get her better. I do need to warn you that she might get nauseous with the medicine, okay?"

"Okay."

"Now the other thing I brought is a Nebulizer, it's to give her breathing treatments. Here again, BJ and Tabitha managed to get ahold of this, so you owe them a big thank you. I also wrote her a prescription for Albuterol. I'll show you how to do all of this, she should have a breathing treatment twice a day, it'll help keep the inflammation in her lungs and airways calm."

Kieran swallowed convulsively, looking terrified. Finley stepped over to the younger woman, taking her hand and giving it a gentle squeeze. "We're going to get her through this as best we can, while avoiding the hospital if at all possible, okay?"

Kieran's tears spilled over. "Thank you so much Finley, I don't know what we'd do without you."

Finley smiled, even though Kieran couldn't see it. "We all love Memphis, she's not allowed to go anywhere."

"Have you heard anything about Remi?" Kieran asked then, knowing that Memphis was likely to ask Finley the first chance she got.

"Wynter told me earlier that she's still on the ventilator. She's staying in close contact with the hospital staff. I know Memphis is probably worried about Remi, but we just have to focus on Memphis' health right now."

"I know," Kieran agreed, "I just wish I could give her good news."

Finley smiled sadly; she'd been hoping that Remi would have improved after five days but that wasn't happening. She, of course, did not share her worry with Kieran. It took a couple of hours to set everything up, explain everything to Memphis, show Kieran everything she needed to do, and write it all down for the young Englishwoman.

Finley finally left the house near midnight, throwing away all of her PPE in their trash before getting into her car town car. Kai still insisted on sending one for her every night that she worked.

"Sorry for the long wait, Sarah," Finley said as she climbed inside.

"No worries, ma'am, how is Memphis doing?" Sarah asked as she started the car.

"Not great right now, but I'm hoping all the stuff I just brought them will help."

"I hope so too," Sarah said, smiling. She'd grown to admire the doctor and her partner, as well as having heard about Memphis and Kieran. It made her feel that she was doing a worthy job at this time of turmoil in the world, making sure a doctor got home safely every night. It gave her a sense of purpose.

Finely dozed in the back seat on the forty-five-minute ride across town, it was much faster than it would have normally been. Since the Stay at Home Order was in place, the streets were eerily empty.

"Ma'am we're here," Sarah said gently, to wake Finley.

"Mmm? Oh, sorry, I dozed off." Finley sat up, seeing that Sarah was holding the door open for her. "Thank you, Sarah," she said as she climbed out of the car, waving as she walked up the driveway. She walked through the side garage door to head into the bathroom to do her usual routine of cleaning up before going into the house.

Half an hour later she crawled into bed with Kai, snuggling up to her. Kai immediately turned over, taking her in her arms and hugging her close.

"How's Memphis?" Kai asked. "Did you get what you were looking for?"

Finley grinned tiredly. "BJ and Tabitha could rule the world from the offices of Wild Irish Silence Studios, I'm tellin' ya."

Kai chuckled, "Well, I'm sure any one of us would have moved heaven and earth to get what Memphis needed."

"Yeah, but BJ has the connections all over the place, I figured it was the best place to start."

"And right you were," Kai murmured leaning in to kiss Finley softly. "That was a very good thing you did, with Memphis."

Finely sighed, "I just couldn't force that poor child into a hospital where I know she's going to be alone and terrified." Tears glazed Finley's eyes even as she said it. "I've seen too many people… die… that way." She choked back the tears as she said the last, the idea of someone she loved dying that way was just a hard knot of terror in her stomach all the time.

"Aw babe…" Kai whispered, hugging Finley closer. "I'm so sorry, I know this is so hard for you. I wish I could help more."

"You're helping," Finley told her, "you're here for me to cry to, you built me my own bathroom! You hired a car to take me to and from work. You cook for me, you do my laundry, you're the most wonderful partner I could have ever imagined."

"You're doing the most important work right now, babe, I have to help you where I can."

"Kai, you need to make sure that Cass is staying safe at school. Can't she just come home?"

"She said something about her roommate going home, and talking to Erin about moving to her room," Kai told her, rolling her eyes at the thought of her sister shacking up with her girlfriend, even if it was in the dorms.

"As long as they're being careful," Finley insisted.

"They are babe, just breathe. You're going to drive yourself crazy worrying about everyone."

Finley took heart in what Kai was saying, feeling the weight of the world on her shoulders at that point but happy to have someone to share it with. She didn't always have what she had now. The younger women she'd dated before meeting Kai would never have understood anything of what she was going through at the hospital, or dealing with her friends being so terribly sick. Kai Templeton understood everything and was the solid rock on which she could rely when things got hard. She loved Kai for that, more than anything at that point.

***

"I can't believe...they did all this..." Memphis managed between deep breaths from the breathing treatment she was doing the next morning after Finley's visit.

"It's pretty amazing," Kieran agreed. "Finley said that this stuff is almost impossible to get ahold of right now, because people are buying up everything."

"And she said BJ did this?" Memphis queried.

"Well, it sounds like Tabitha helped him, but yes, he paid for it all."

Memphis shook her head in wonder. "I might have to do another album for him," she mused as she finished up the treatment.

Kieran rolled her eyes at her wife, "I'm sure that's not why he did this."

"Probably not," Memphis acquiesced, "but I'll still feel indebted to him, to Fin too."

"Everyone just wants you to feel better," Kieran told her, "how *are* you feeling?"

Memphis chewed on the inside of her lower lip, her look assessing. "I think I'm relieved more than anything right now," she admitted, "I still feel super tired and all, but I think the breathing stuff is helping."

"Good," Kieran smiled, "we need to do your IV after lunch, and Finley did want you to try and eat something today if you can manage." Memphis grimaced, looking highly unenthusiastic about that idea. "I know you don't want to, love, but Finley says that with the weight you've lost over the last few weeks, you're almost too underweight for this Remdesivir. She wants some food in your system before we do the IV." Kieran purposely left out the part about the medicine possibly causing Memphis to feel nauseous.

Memphis sniffed wanting to complain, but knowing she had no right to. She was being taken care of by someone she loved in her own home. Not stuck by herself in some hospital ward, being tended to by strangers.

"Okay, I'll try to eat," she finally agreed.

"Good." Kieran smiled.

After a lunch of soup and half a grilled cheese sandwich, Kieran used the IV port Finley had put in Memphis' forearm the night before to start the IV of medicine. They watched a movie while it ran its course, but Memphis slept off and on the entire time. When the IV bag was empty, Kieran carefully removed the tube and closed off the port, doing her best not to wake Memphis.

She hoped that if there was any nausea, Memphis would sleep through it. In the end, Memphis slept the rest of the day.

Chapter 3

3,039 Cases/ 9 Deaths in California
179,767 Cases Worldwide/4,994 Deaths

March 13, 2020

Four days later Riley couldn't stand it any longer, she was sick of room service and just wanted some fresh fruits and vegetables. Putting her hair under a baseball cap and donning large sunglasses, Riley left the room for the first time in two weeks. The lobby of the hotel that had previously been bustling was empty. She was surprised when one of the hotel employees trotted over to her handing her a blue paper mask, saying, "è obbligatorio" apologetically.

Riley nodded, doing her best to put on the strange paper mask. It immediately slid upwards, partially covering her glasses. The hotel employee, who was wearing disposable gloves, held up his hand to her then reached over, pulling down the mask over her chin and pinching the wire at her nose.

"Oh, grazie," Riley nodded, feeling a bit foolish for not knowing how to deal with the mask.

"Non c'è problema." the man nodded; his own face covered with a black cloth mask. "Dove sono i tuoi documenti?"

Riley understood the first part but canted her head on the second. Holding up her hands, she said, "Non capisco," indicating that she didn't understand.

"Your papers," the man said.

Riley didn't understand what he meant, assuming he meant her passport, so she patted her purse. He nodded, "Sì buono."

Leaving the hotel, Riley was shocked at how empty the streets were. It was noon and the pavements were usually filled with people, but today it was so eerily quiet that it made her shiver involuntarily. She made her way down the street, feeling uncomfortable in the strange hush all around her. She was a couple of blocks from the hotel when a car pulled up next to her. Somewhat surprised that the car had pulled up so close to her, she stopped and looked over. It was a police car. Two men got out, one moving to stand in front of her, holding up his hands to keep her from continuing forward.

"Cosa ci fai fuori di casa?" the officer demanded.

Riley shook her head, not understanding the question. "Inglese?" she queried.

"Americano?" the man snapped.

"Sì." Riley nodded, trying to ignore the man's attitude.

The man launched into what sounded like a tirade—it included one word that she recognized: "stupido." When it was clear the man in front of her thought she was some stupid American, Riley got angry.

"I am not stupid just because I don't speak fluent Italian, you jerk!" she yelled.

The man raised his voice, gesturing with his hands wildly.

Riley crossed her arms in front of her chest and looked back at the man, refusing to be intimidated by him. That seemed to only infuriate him more. He grabbed her arm and started shoving her toward the car. Wrenching her arm away from the man, Riley glared at him.

"What do you think you're doing!" she screamed. "You have no right to grab me like that!"

Finally, the other officer moved into view, putting himself between Riley and the other man. He too held up his hands, but in more of a calming gesture, putting his palms down and making a pushing motion as if trying to lower the tension physically.

"We just need to know why you are out of your home, lady," the second officer said. His English was heavily accented, but at least Riley could understand him.

"I'm going to the market," Riley told him, her tone still a bit haughty. She could almost hear Legend in her head saying *calm down babe, you'll get yourself arrested...* "That's still legal right?" she queried angrily.

"Yes lady, but do you have your paper?"

"My what?" Riley asked, remembering the hotel employee asking that question too.

"I tuoi documenti! Documenti!" the other officer yelled, throwing up his hands in a gesture of futility.

Riley pulled her passport out of her purse handing it to the calmer officer. The man looked at the document and Riley knew the moment that he recognized her. She would have sworn she heard it actually click in his head. His eyes widened, as he looked from the passport to Riley; she took off her glassed and took down the paper mask to oblige his identification. Sometimes it paid to be a worldwide well-known star.

"Riley Taylor?" the officer queried in a halting awed voice.

"Riley Taylor?" the angry officer echoed.

"Yes, that's me," Riley said, doing her best not to bat her eyelashes as she did.

Both officers started nodding, looking starstruck.

It took another few minutes of signing autographs and posing for selfies, and then Riley was on her way again. She made it to the store and was surprised to have to wait in a line before being let into the store. Having donned her glasses and mask again, no one recognized her, and she was fine with that being the case. The man standing at the front of the store looked like the bouncer at a bar, and he certainly seemed to be keeping track of everyone that went into the store. He was only letting people in one at a time. Riley did her best to stay back from the other people in line and wait her turn.

Even the market turned out to be a rather eerie experience. With no people to smile at or nod to, Riley felt more alone than ever. By the time she arrived back at her hotel room with her small bag of fruits and vegetables, as well as a bottle of wine she'd picked up at a store on her route back, she was exhausted. Crawling into bed, she turned on the TV and simply stared at it for the rest of the day, falling asleep early. This became her pattern over the next week or so. She rarely ate, and even her phone calls to Legend became shorter and shorter.

***

"When was this blood work done?" the doctor on rounds asked Cynthia.

"This morning, doctor," the nurse answered as she glanced at her watch, was it really already one thirty in the afternoon?

"I don't like her platelet count. Let's run it again. How has her urine output been?"

Cynthia grimaced, "Only two hundred in the last twenty-four hours."

"Draw her blood and tell the lab we need the platelet count quickly," the doctor ordered.

An hour later, Remi's oxygen levels were dropping dangerously, and the doctor's fears had been proven by the blood results. Cynthia called Wynter.

"How's she doing?" Wynter answered her phone with a smile, expecting to hear good news, Remi was a fighter.

"I'm afraid she's much worse this afternoon." Cynthia's voice conveyed her unhappiness at having to convey such bad news. "She's showing signs of sepsis."

"What is that?"

"It's an infection in her blood stream. It's very dangerous."

"Is she…" Wynter began, tears beginning to clog her throat. "Is she dying?" It was unimaginable, Remi couldn't die, but people were dying all over the world because of this virus.

She heard it was up to almost 5,000 people and scientists were speculating it would get much, much worse before it got better. This was just the "beginning" according to them. The estimates were that millions would die before this virus was done; it was unimaginable in this day and age! Every day more people were getting sick, over 130,000 already. What right did she have to think that her wife would be one of the people who wouldn't die?

"I wish I had better news," Cynthia couldn't say whether or not Remington LaRoché would die, but she knew that her chances had dropped significantly over the last twenty-four hours.

"Please let me know if anything changes," Wynter told the nurse, "We're just a few minutes from the hospital. I can come right down if needed."

Unfortunately, Cynthia had to remind her that she wouldn't be able to be at Remi's bedside in the event that things became more serious. Wynter fell asleep that night with the heart wrenching thought that she may never hold Remi's hand again, or see her smile, or hear her laugh. Her pillow grew wet with her tears.

When Wynter's phone rang the next morning, she felt sick instantly.

"You need to come down, now," Cynthia told her.

Quinn escorted her into the hospital and up to the ICU. There they were able to stand outside the window and see Remi in the hospital bed with tubes and IVs running into her arms, not to mention the ventilator tube.

"Holy shyte..." Quinn breathed, grimacing.

Wynter drew her breath in through her nose, trying desperately not to burst into tears. She saw Cynthia in the room, she was holding up her cell phone and pointing to Wynter as Wynter's phone rang. Wynter answered and Cynthia put the phone she was holding up to Remi's ear, even though Remi was still in the coma.

Wynter knew this could be her last chance to communicate with Remi.

"Hi babe," Wynter said softly, "I know that you're probably tired by now, that this has been one seriously long round, but I really need you to keep fighting, okay? I love you so much, and don't even want to begin imagining my life without you, so you need to push through."

"What are you doing here?" her friend Jack was asking her.

"I'm here for the fight," Remi told him.

"The fight's been canceled, you can just rest now," Jack told her.

"But…" Remi's voice trailed off as Jack's face morphed into Akasha's.

"You tired bitch?" Akasha taunted nastily. "You just lay down, or I'll beat that ass some more!"

"I am ready to fight," Remi told her, but her arms felt so heavy, and she was so tired suddenly. "I am…" she began again, doing her best to respond to Akasha's taunts.

"You ain't got nothing left, LaRoachie!" Akasha sneered. "You're a washed-up old has-been! Just lay there and die!" Suddenly Akasha had her hands on Remi's mouth, she was keeping her from breathing!

I have to breathe! Remi thought, panicking as the urge to breathe became stronger. I can't, I can't… so tired… Akasha was kneeling on her chest now, smashing her hands into Remi's mouth and throat. Remi reached up, grabbing at Akasha's hands, but they weren't hands, they were… that snake, it was back!

Remi began to move, grimacing, her hands pulling against the restraints. It was terrifying to watch. Cynthia quickly set the phone down and moved to extract medicine from a file on a nearby table.

"What's happening!" Wynter called into the phone.

"She's coming out of the sedation! Her breathing is so labored, I'm trying to re-sedate her," Cynthia called out, even as she reached over and hit a panic button for the room. A tone sounded and staff started moving toward the room. Wynter and Quinn were told they needed to leave.

Outside in the car, Wynter cried in Quinn's arms.

"What if that's the last time I see her?" she lamented, "I can't do this…" Wynter shook her head, starting to gasp for breath.

"Easy now," Quinn told her, recognizing the signs of a panic attack. She'd talked Xandy through a few of them in their time together. "Just breathe slowly."

"I have to get back in there!" Wynter exclaimed, moving to reach for the door handle.

"They won't let you in, Wyn, you know that," Quinn reasoned.

"I don't care! I have to talk to her I have to get to her!" Wynter cried trying to get to the door, but Quinn held her back.

"Wynter wait!" Quinn grappled with the smaller woman. "If you try to force your way in there – Stop!" Quinn yelled sharply now, because Wynter was going to get herself hurt. "If you try to force your way in there," she repeated, holding Wynter firmly bey the shoulders, "you're going to have security on you, and then I'm going to have to step in. Do you want me to get hurt?"

"You don't have to step in," Wynter told her.

"I do have to step in," Quinn assured her, "I have to protect you, not only because BJ is counting on me, but so is Remi."

Wynter bit back a retort, her contorting with sorrow and anguish. "I can't lose her..." she whispered fiercely.

Quinn nodded, hugging Wynter to her again. The idea of Remi dying was killing Quinn too, they'd become good friends, bonding over the protection of their ladies. It was terrifying to think that someone so strong could be killed by this virus, it didn't bear thinking about.

They stayed in the car until Cynthia called Wynter and told her that they'd stabilized Remi's breathing, but that it would be better if Wynter went home. The danger had passed for the moment. In her heart, Wynter knew that Cynthia purposely didn't offer a lot of hope, because there wasn't a lot the doctors could do at that point. They'd been trying different medications in different doses to combat the virus ravaging Remi's body.

March 14, 2020

After two days of waiting and worrying every time the phone rang, Wynter got a call from Cynthia. It took her an extra few moments to answer because she was terrified that Cynthia would tell her Remi was dead.

"Yes?" Wynter answered finally.

"She's doing a bit better today, we've inserted a central line to give her blood pressure medication."

"Why?" Wynter asked.

"Her blood pressure was getting dangerously high after a few of her waking episodes, so we wanted to bring that back down. We're monitoring her very closely, I assure you."

"Thank you so much," Wynter said, still feeling a bit sick at the idea of Remi's blood pressure being high and wondering what damage that could cause. She asked Finley later that day.

"Well, I can promise you," Finley told her frankly, "that they're doing the right thing. High blood pressure can lead to a stroke or a heart attack, and we definitely don't want that on top of everything else."

Wynter blew her breath out, doing her best not to freak out every time someone brought up something else that scared the living daylights out of her. "Okay."

"Did they say it was working?" Finley asked.

"Yes, she said that Remi's blood pressure was stabilizing."

"That's good," Finley assured her, "at this point with this virus, we doctors are just trying to treat things as they come up. If someone tries something new, we're putting it out there for everyone's knowledge. No one is hiding info on this virus, so keep the faith, Wynter."

Wynter smiled through the tears gathering in her eyes. "Thank you Fin, I wish you were here to treat Remi yourself, but I'm glad to hear that doctors are working together on this."

"And how are you?" Finley asked. "Are you taking care of yourself?"

Wynter glanced up as there was a light knock on her door and Xandy walked in carrying a tray with dinner on it.

"Xandy is taking care of me and Quinn," Wynter said, smiling at the younger girl. "Don't worry."

"Good! And they're both healthy?"

"Yes," Wynter nodded, "how is everyone there, how's Memphis?"

"Mostly everyone here is good. Memphis is doing much better."

"I'm so glad. The last thing I wanted to have to tell Remi is anything bad about Memphis. She felt bad enough that she could be there for her during all of this craziness."

"Well, you can tell her that Memphis is fine, and that she is now free to get better herself." Wynter could hear the wink in Finley's voice and appreciated it.

"I'll tell her just that," Wynter said, "well, I better go, my dinner is getting cold. Thank you again Fin, love you. My love to Kai, give her a hug for me."

"Will do. Love you too, we'll keep sending good thoughts Remi's way. You all take care too."

After she'd hung up with Finley, Wynter felt better. Taking her dinner out to the dining room, she joined Quinn and Xandy.

"What did Fin have to say?" Quinn asked.

"She said that the doctors are doing the smart thing," Wynter told them.

"Good." Xandy smiled. "It's good to hear that from someone we trust."

"Yeah," Wynter nodded, as she took a bite of her bread, "Fin told me that the doctors are all sharing information on this virus as they find things that work or try new stuff. So that's pretty cool."

"Definitely," Quinn agreed.

Over the next four days, they repeated the breathing treatments and use of the Remdesivir and slowly but surely, Memphis got better. On her final day of the Remdesivir, she received a package in the mail from BJ. Inside a box wrapped in rainbow paper was a rose gold iPad Air and the moment she pulled it out of the box it lit up with an incoming video call. Memphis answered it with a silly grin on her face, she was not surprised to see BJ's face on the screen.

"There she is!" BJ exclaimed. "How are you feeling my little love?"

Memphis couldn't help but smile at BJ's endearment. "I'm doing good, BJ, thank you so much for everything you've done for me."

BJ waved aside her gratitude, "I consider you one of my own, and there's nothing I won't do for one of my own."

Memphis pressed her lips together as tears came to her eyes. Because she didn't trust her voice, she nodded to him. She didn't know what she'd done to earn this man's loyalty, but she was very grateful for it.

"So you're feeling better?" BJ asked. "That medicine that Finley put you on is working?"

"I think so," Memphis said, "my oxygen levels are up, my fever is gone, so I really think it is."

"Excellent!" I'm really happy to hear that."

"Have you heard anything about Remi?" Memphis asked.

BJ grimaced, shaking his head. "Not really, no, Remi is still in the coma at this point. I'm sorry I don't have better news."

"It's not your fault," Memphis said, "this virus sucks."

"You can say that again!" BJ told her. They spoke for a while longer, but BJ didn't want to wear her out. "By the way, I gave everyone this number and an iPad of their own, so they could have video visits with you. Figured you could use the cheering up and so could they."

"You are the most awesome man on the planet," Memphis told him, sincerity strong in her voice.

"Considering how little you think of men, I'll take that as a big compliment." BJ winked. "You take good care little love."

"You and Allex stay safe too and tell Tabbie thank you from me too!"

"You got it," BJ agreed.

After they disconnected, Memphis held up the iPad Air to Kieran. "Do you know how much these things cost?" Kieran shook her head. "Like eight hundred bucks!" Memphis exclaimed. "BJ is crazy!"

"I think he loves you and wants to make sure you can stay in touch with people."

"Yeah, but this is…" Memphis said, her eyes gazing at the beauty that was the newest iPad. "This is the coolest thing ever."

Kieran smiled, thinking to herself (not for the first time since she'd met him) that Brenden James Sparks had some serious style and the biggest heart of gold.

In the days that followed, Memphis got an opportunity to catch up with the rest of the group. It helped her to continue to get better, while staying at home. The video chats made things feel a little normal.

Four days later Midnight Chevalier declared a Shelter in Place order, telling Californians to stay home unless they had to go to work or shopping for essentials like food and groceries. It was a sign that things had just gotten very serious in California and that the Governor was going to great lengths to attempt to illustrate that to the citizens. Thanks to Finley, all the members of the group were fully aware of how grave the situation with COVID was, it was important the Midnight show others.

For people like Memphis, staying at home wasn't really a problem, but things like staying in touch with her friends was tantamount so sanity. The video chats became everyone's lifeline.

March 19, 2020

"Aren't you overreacting a bit?" the reporter with the bad combover asked.

"When the WHO says there's a pandemic, I believe them," Midnight fired back.

She'd just announced the Statewide Stay at Home order, and people were naturally in shock. The reporters were like sharks in a feeding frenzy.

"What about businesses? And schools!" another reporter cried.

"We have to see how things go, right now, we're being told that this virus spreads quick and is much more deadly than the flu and we need to treat it as such. Until we can get more widespread testing and slow this thing down, this is what we need to do."

There were many more questions hurled her way and, as usual, Midnight handled them all, doing her best to keep down her ire. She knew that the last thing people wanted was to have to stay home and not be allowed to go out to their favorite places. What she also knew, however, was that she didn't want to be responsible for millions of dead Californians.

"They seriously think I'm overreacting!" Midnight exclaimed on the way back to their hotel that afternoon.

"People are scared and confused babe," Rick told her, "they'll understand eventually."

Midnight pressed her lips together in annoyance, "You sure about that?"

"No," Rick admitted, already knowing this was going to a be a rough ride, "but I have to hope that people are smart enough listen to someone not talking out of both sides of their mouth."

Midnight sighed, pressing her forehead against the cool glass of the passenger window. She understood what Rick meant, they were getting zero consistency or true support from the White House, and Midnight truly felt it was up to her to save California.

"This is gonna suck," she muttered.

***

It was late at night when Riley heard the fire alarm go off in the hotel. Doing her best not to panic, she got out of bed and pulled on clothes and shoes. As she moved out into the hallway crowds of people did the same. She did her best to stay away from people as she realized that hardly any of them wore masks. Fortunately, she still had a mask shoved in the pocket of her jacket, so she was able to don that as they headed down the stairwell. She was jostled and bumped and did her best to keep her footing, but then someone panicked and started running down the stairs, knocking her down as they did. Falling, she caught herself thinking, *am I going to get trampled in all of this?* That was her last thought as her head hit the wall and she was knocked unconscious.

March 20, 2020

Riley woke slowly. Her head hurt and it took her a few long moments to remember what had happened. As she opened her eyes she knew she wasn't at the hotel; looking around she noticed older antique furniture, and there was a lovely breeze coming in from the open window near the bed she lay on.

"Where the Hell am I?" Riley muttered to herself as she moved to sit up, her feet touching the cold terracotta floor.

Almost as if on cue a young woman dressed in a red skirt and white peasant style shirt came rushing into the room.

"Facile perdere," the young woman said in Italian. "Easy," she repeated, when she realized that Riley didn't understand her. "You are hurt."

"Where am I?" Riley demanded, feeling her head start to pound.

"Si prega di perdere," the young woman rushed to Riley's side trying to encourage her to lay back down. "Please singora, I will be in big trouble. Please!"

"Okay, okay," Riley said, moving to lay back since her head was now demanding that she lay down before she blacked out again. "Please, just tell me where I am."

When the young woman saw that Riley was complying, she stepped back. "You are in the home of la mia signora, my lady, she is called Francesca Ferrara."

"Francesca Ferrara," Riley repeated in disbelief. Francesca Ferrara was a wildly famous Italian actress, and someone of great influence in the film world. At thirty, she was much younger than Riley but she'd made a number of movies that had been critically acclaimed.

"Si," the young woman nodded, "I am called Eva. Are you hungry?"

Riley looked back at Eva in disbelief. "Seriously? You think you're gonna drop that bomb and then just move on to lunch? *Why* am I here? How did I get here? What the hell is going on! Ouch!" The last was said because raising her voice hurt.

"Ma'am, please do not be mad with me, my lady she will come to talk with you soon."

"Then go get her," Riley told the girl succinctly.

Eva widened her big dark eyes but then nodded, not wanting to anger the American any more than she already seemed to be. She left the room in a hurry.

Riley closed her eyes, feeling her head thudding dully. She had no idea what was going on, but she intended to find out. Had she been kidnapped? Why on Earth would a famous actress want to kidnap her? It made no sense at all.

It was another hour before the actress herself swept into the room. Riley hated her immediately. The woman was beyond beautiful: with her long dark curly hair, perfect olive skin and dark sultry brown eyes she was youth and vitality embodied. It was depressing. Riley sat up warily.

"I see you have awakened," Francesca breathed, her Italian accent making every word sound sexy.

"Yeah, like an hour ago," Riley snapped. "Why the hell am I here?"

Francesca's eyes widened at Riley's tone. "My men brought you here."

Riley's eyes narrowed, "You say that like that explains everything."

Francesca pressed her lips together, giving Riley the ingénue smile she was famous for, which only irritated Riley more.

"We got you out of Rome, things there were getting out of hand."

"Out of hand how?"

"It was far too restrictive for people like us," Francesca explained.

"Like us?" Riley repeated woodenly.

"People who need to run wild and free," Francesca said spreading her arms wide.

"So you kidnapped me?"

"Kidnapped? No mia cara." Francesca looked horrified by the thought. "My people came to the hotel, but the hotel staff would not tell them where you were." She shrugged delicately. "They decided to get creative and activated the fire alarm. But that did not go as planned."

"Ya think?" Riley snapped, gesturing to the lump on her forehead.

"I am so very sorry!" Francesca assured her, moving to sit on the bed. "When you did not come out of the hotel they went in and found you lying in the stairwell. They brought you here and the doctor came to see you and said you were okay."

Riley shook her head, "Okay, but how did you know I was there? How did you even know who I am?"

Francesca looked shocked, "Who would not know who you are? You are famous, the Riley Taylor!"

Riley did her best not to let her ego fluff her up too much. "Still, you technically kidnapped me."

"Ah, si," Francesca nodded, "but Legend said you would be happier out here in the country with us."

"Legend?" Riley replied dumbly.

"Si! Legend called me and begged a favor."

Riley shook her head. "Legend did this."

"She is very persuasive," Francesca sighed dreamily.

Riley's eyes narrowed again. "She is, huh?"

"Oh yes, I adore her, so she can talk me into anything."

"I'll bet," Riley quipped, knowing without a doubt that Legend had slept with this woman. Legend had been well known for sleeping with the leading ladies in her films.

Fortunately, Francesca was called away at that point, so Riley didn't get a chance to find out what all Legend had convinced her of in the past. After resting for a while, Riley's curiosity got the better of her—as well as her growling stomach. She wandered out of the room and smelled the heavenly scent of baking bread; she followed that scent all the way to the kitchen.

The house itself had a very comfortable feel to it, with terracotta tiled floors throughout. The décor felt very rustic, not overbearing or fancy by any means. She passed through a living room with large, overstuffed couches in white and beige. The walls were decorated with understated artwork. The ceilings were rough-hewn wood, doorways were curved and accented with bare red brick. Riley couldn't help but admire the easy feel to the house, it seemed like a wonderful getaway. She'd hoped it would be awful and she could at least point to bad taste on the part of the Italian actress, but that hope was dashed with every room she walked through.

When she finally made it to the kitchen, she encountered Eva again. The maid was happy to cut her some bread and provide butter and homemade jam as well. Riley didn't think she'd ever tasted anything so wonderful in her life. The bread was still warm and the butter tasted so fresh, the jam was a delight as well. Eva even poured her a glass of Pinot Grigio wine that was the perfect complement to the bread: it tasted of citrus with a warm honeyed quality to it.

"This is fabulous!" Riley exclaimed to Eva. "What brand is this wine?"

"It is bottled here on the vineyard," Eva told her, noting Riley's change of tone from earlier in the day.

"Wow," Riley was duly impressed, "I think I need to check this out."

Eva happily walked Riley down to the vineyards, and even introduced her to the viticoltore, the man responsible for the management of the wine making process. Luca Caruso was a boisterous man in his fifties, with a large round belly and a deep baritone laugh. Riley liked him immediately. He happily gave her a tour of the vineyards and allowed her to sample many of the wines they made there. Riley had a new favorite, the brand was called Caruso Ferrara, Riley had to begrudgingly give Francesca more points for allowing the maker's name before hers.

That evening dinner was a whole other culinary experience. Francesca's chef made a wonderful multi course meal including a fresh caprese salad of various heirloom tomatoes grown in the garden, freshly made mozzarella cheese, herbs and olive oil. There was more baked bread, a wonderful carbonara, as well as Italian Wedding soup. Riley didn't think she'd ever eaten so much in her life—or drank more wine.

It turned out that Francesca was actually a fairly good conversationalist. They discussed current events, as well as exchanged tales from the Italian movie sets.

"Aw but the men they are always easy to manage, right?" Francesca laughed as she waved her had airily.

"Yes, yes they are," Riley agreed. "So what have you been doing since they've closed everything down?"

"They have asked me to help with the townspeople."

"Help?" Riley echoed, her look slightly horrified. "Doing what?"

Francesca laughed, wagging her finger at Riley, "No, no, not like nursing, I am far from, how you say, equipped for that! I have been working with the Radioaudizioni Italiane."

"The what?" Riley asked dumbly.

"The, aw, radio broadcasters, talking to people about this virus."

"Oh, you mean like PSAs," Riley nodded. "Public Service Announcements," she clarified when Francesca gave her a blank look at the acronym.

"Aw, si, si, helping people understand and be safe."

"It's good that you can do that," Riley told her.

Francesca shrugged. "It is what I can do."

Riley nodded, realizing that the Italian movie star was just as human as the rest of them, and doing what she could in this unprecedented time.

"So, how well do you know Legend?" Riley asked slyly.

Francesca pressed her lips together in a coquettish smile. "You are the one that caught her," was all she'd say.

In the end, it was a lovely night.

That night it began to rain, and Riley lay listening to the raindrops hitting the tiles in the courtyard just outside of her room. She fell asleep to that sound. She woke to the feel of someone touching her cheek.

Her eyes flew open, expecting to take someone to task for having the nerve to touch her so intimately! Riley was stunned to be staring into the hazel eyes of her wife.

"Legend?" she whispered, shocked.

Legend smiled. "Hey there beautiful."

Riley moved to sit up and threw herself forward into Legend's arms. "Oh my God, oh my God!" she chanted as she hugged Legend fiercely. "How are you here?"

"Talent?" Legend queried with a rakish grin.

Riley moved back to give Legend a sour look. "Talent, huh? Did that have to include one of your old conquest's?

"Maybe?" Legend grimaced, opening one eye to give her wife a sidelong look.

"And why exactly did you have me sent to her homes of all places?"

Legend chuckled good naturedly, having known it wouldn't take long for Riley to nail her with that one.

"Well, babe," Legend said, putting her index finger to the bridge of her nose and rubbing it absently, "she's the only one I knew of with an airstrip big enough to fit Joe Sinclair's plane, and where the air traffic control could be bribed to ignore a single plane entering Italian airspace during a pandemic lockdown."

"Oh," Riley replied lamely, looking embarrassed about her ire.

"I was worried about you, babe," Legend told her, reaching out to take Riley's hand.

"Now how am I supposed to be mad at you?" Riley muttered.

Legend laughed, moving to stand and pull her wife into her arms again, hugging her close. "You're not supposed to be mad at me," Legend informed her, "you're supposed to be happy that I rode in on a white stallion, okay, plane, to rescue you."

"Rescue me, huh?"

"Indeed," Legend answered, leaning down to kiss Riley's lips.

"Mmm…" Riley hummed against Legend's lips. "No one's ever rescued me before."

"I like being original." Legend laughed.

"Yes, yes you do!" Riley agreed, so happy suddenly, she couldn't believe Legend was actually standing in front of her. "Wait! I'm not dreaming, am I?"

"Let's find out…" Legend murmured as she kicked off her boots and shed her jacket, taking her wife into her arms, beginning to kiss her neck.

Riley sighed, letting her head fall back and thoroughly enjoyed her wonderful, handsome boi's attention. Legend slowly shifted the silky nightgown Riley wore up to her hips, as she moved lower, eliciting moans of pleasure from her wife. It had been so long since they'd been together, that it took no time at all for Riley to orgasm, her hands grasping Legend's hair in her release. Once Riley calmed down, Legend moved up slightly, resting her head on Riley's stomach and enjoying the feel of her wife's skin. Riley's hands were still in her hair, stroking and letting her nails graze Legend's scalp. They lay together quietly for a long while, just enjoying being near each other again.

"So what happens now?" Riley asked.

"I'm thinking sleep…" Legend grinned lazily.

Riley clicked her tongue. "I meant tomorrow, or I guess it's today, later though, you know, when it's daylight and all."

Legend chuckled. "Well," she moved so that she lay next to Riley, and Riley readily moved into her arms, glancing up at her. "I brought a COVID test with me, sent by Finley," Legend's lips pressed together in a slight grimace, "her exact words, 'don't you bring another case of COVID home to me!' So, we're going to have you take the test, and 'cesca will give it to the doctor she had look you over when you got here. If you're negative, then we can fly home as soon as you want."

"'Cesca, huh?" Riley repeated sourly. "I'm not sure I like that you have a pet name for her."

Legend looked back at Riley adroitly, "Seriously? You're still mad about that?"

"I'm jealous, not mad," Riley qualified.

Legend gave a short chuckle. "Okay. So, in the meantime, we can just relax and enjoy each other."

"But then we can go home," Riley clarified.

"But then we can go home," Legend confirmed.

The next morning, after the jarring experience of the COVID test, Legend and Riley had breakfast with Francesca and Riley found that Legend was quite adept at keeping things friendly. There were a few instances where Francesca would foray into the area of Legend's prowess or how handsome she was, but Legend would always steer the conversation back to a safer topic. To her credit Francesca picked up the cues quickly, like any good actress, and adjusted accordingly.

Later that morning, Legend surprised Riley by taking her horseback riding. It wasn't something Riley had done in many years. They had a great time, spending the day exploring the Tuscan countryside, fortunately Francesca's property was vast, so they were perfectly safe and only encountered a few field hands on their journey. Francesca's chef had prepared them a wonderful picnic lunch that included a couple of different wines, various cheeses, some cold chicken as well as an antipasto salad and some fresh bread.

"This is pure heaven!" Riley exclaimed, leaning back and letting the sun warm her face.

"So, not pure hell?" Legend asked as she broke off another piece of cheese.

"Oh stop!" Riley gave her a sour look. "I never said it was pure hell, Francesca is perfectly lovely, it's just my jealous streak that's causing the problem."

"So stop being jealous," Legend offered, "you're the one I married."

Riley considered Legend's words. "True," she agreed after a long moment.

"Glad we got that settled," Legend said, handing Riley her glass of wine.

"I love this wine!" Riley enthused.

"Yeah, it's pretty damned good." Legend nodded as she sipped her wine.

"Maybe we should buy a house here."

"In Italy?" Legend looked shocked.

"For when we retire," Riley told her.

"We're retiring?" Legend's eyebrow arched in her curiosity.

"Eventually!" Riley exclaimed. "And it's so beautiful here."

Legend nodded, thinking that her wife was definitely feeling the wine she'd been drinking.

March 25, 2020

The days that followed were a rollercoaster of emotions. Remi's blood pressure went up, then they brought it down with meds. Her oxygen levels would be steady, and they'd drop suddenly, creating an emergency. There were a couple more trips down to the hospital thinking she might be seeing Remi for the last time. Wynter's nerves were stretched thin as she did her best to be brave, like she knew Remi would want her to be.

What is happening?

"You're dying," a voice said.

"Who are you?" Remi asked trying to look around, but it was too dark to see.

"It doesn't matter. Soon your body will give out and you will die," the voice told her matter of factly.

"I don't want to die."

"That doesn't matter either," the voice sighed. "Besides you believe in Fate, maybe I'm Fate and I'm telling you what's in your future."

"I don't believe that."

"What do you believe?" The voice asked.

"That you are a dyab that is trying to take away my hope."

"A devil? Me?" the voice laughed, a far from happy sound. "Maybe I am, maybe you deserve what's coming to you!"

Remi recognized the voice now, it was Akasha, how had she been changing her voice?

"O se ou menm, it's just you, Akasha. You will not say when I die," Remi said, her voice stronger now that she knew her enemy.

"You're dying Remi, get used to the idea!" Akasha insisted.

"I am not," Remi replied, even as the darkness began to lighten. "I am going to live, and you nor anyone else will stop that."

"Oh my lord, look at those levels!" Cynthia exclaimed to her co-worker. "Go get the doctor!"

Half an hour later, Wynter got a phone call.

"Come now!" Cynthia told her.

"Oh my God, I can't…" Wynter shook her head.

"Wynter, she's better! Much, much better! We're weaning her off the sedation!"

Wynter's mouth dropped open, and she was sure she was going to faint, blinking slowly as she tried to take in what Cynthia was saying. Quinn moved to her side, seeing her dumbfounded look.

"What is it?" the Irishwoman asked.

"It's Remi…" Wynter whispered.

"What…" Quinn asked, looking sick suddenly too.

Wynter saw the look on Quinn's face and shook her head immediately as she came out of her daze. "No! Quinn, she's doing better! We need to get down there!"

A half an hour later Wynter walked into the ICU with Quinn on her heels. Cynthia saw them and hastened over.

"She's doing really well now. She's not completely out of the woods, but they are bringing her out of the coma, and she'll likely be taken off the ventilator in a few days."

Quinn put her arm around Wynter's shoulders, hugging her close.

"That's such awesome news, thank you so much!" Wynter nodded, her blue eyes shimmering with tears of joy.

"I'm rather chuffed about it too!" Cynthia exclaimed.

"Too right!" Quinn added, her Irish accent clear.

"I best be getting back," Cynthia told them, "of course she won't be able to talk until the breathing tube comes out, but I'll give her back her phone and she can at least text you as soon as she able."

"That would be wonderful!" Wynter enthused.

March 26, 2020

The texts started the next day. They were a bit disjointed at first, but Wynter didn't care, she was just so happy to hear from Remi that she was beside herself. When Remi's texts became more understandable, Wynter suggested that she text Memphis to let her know that she was doing better. She'd explained via text that Memphis was much better and that later on when she was off the ventilator, they could do a video chat with Memphis.

In California, Memphis' phone pinged while she was carrying groceries that had been delivered to their doorstep into the house. In the kitchen, Kieran was putting things away. Memphis set down the grocery bag and pulled out her phone. She was stunned to see a text from Remi.

"Oh my dawg!" Memphis exclaimed so loudly it made Kieran jump.

"What! You scared the life out of me!"

"Sorry! I just got a text from Remi!"

"What does it say?" Kieran asked, immediately as excited as Memphis was.

"Remington LaRoché back in service," Memphis read, laughing, "she's been hanging out with the cops too long!" She texted Remi back just that.

The reply came back: "Wi!"

"So happy you're doing better," Memphis said as she texted Remi back, saying it out loud so Kieran knew what she was telling Remi.

"Hear you are better too," came the reply.

"Much better, thanks to Fin," Memphis answered.

It was a short conversation, but it made Memphis' day.

March 29, 2020

"There she is…" Wynter murmured into the phone she held up to her ear as she watched Remi's eyes open slowly. They were on Facetime.

"Hey," Remi croaked, her voice extremely hoarse from the breathing tube that had been removed that morning, four hours before.

"Your voice will get better as your vocal cords heal," Cynthia told Remi, she was the one holding the phone out to Remi with the speaker on.

"Remi, that's Cynthia, she took really good care of you over the last three or so weeks," Wynter told her.

"Three?" Remi managed to say.

"Yes, twenty-three days actually," Wynter told her, grimacing slightly, "but you're better now and that's what really counts babe." Remi nodded slowly. She moved to reach up to scratch her

105

cheek and looked very dismayed suddenly. "What is it babe?" Wynter asked.

"Weak," Remi said.

Wynter drew in a deep breath, nodding as she did. "Yeah, you'll be that way for a while, but we'll get you back to normal, don't worry."

Again, Remi nodded slowly, looking tired again already.

"Okay, I can see you're getting worn out," Wynter told her, "I'm going to let you rest for now, but we can talk again later. You know you can call me whenever you want, okay? Or text, use that talk to text feature, it'll be easier at this point."

"Love…you," Remi told her.

"I love you," Wynter smiled brightly, "I've missed you so much babe, but you're better and that's what matters. Everyone is so happy for you, and they all send their love."

"Love…them…too."

"I'll tell them you said so. Rest now babe."

April 1, 2020

"It that an April Fool's joke?" Midnight asked her secretary.

"No ma'am, that was the message," Chris told her.

Midnight looked at the message again, reading it out loud. "Need more PPE." Then she looked at her long-time assistant again. "What's PPE?"

"I looked it up, it's Personal Protective Equipment, so masks, gowns, gloves, stuff like that."

"Sheesh, you could have written that on here," Midnight grinned.

"Sorry ma'am, I wrote the message before I looked it up," Chris grimaced.

"Not totally your fault, I guess I really need to get up to speed on this part of being the Governor. Let's find out how much we have, and how much we need, so we can get on ordering it. I imagine it's getting harder and harder to find, like toilet paper is right now. Too bad the Feds won't be much help."

April 10, 2020

Remi finally got to the point where she could breathe without the assistance of oxygen, and she could carry on a conversation. She'd had many video chats with the group, especially with Memphis. It was shocking to Remi when she realized how much weight she'd lost, and how very weak she was. She couldn't walk without a walker, but she was determined to work on that.

"I'll whip you back into shape when you get home," Kai had told her, "just get your ass home Marine!"

"Bon Bondye! I have to get out of the hospital first!"

"You need to build up your strength and we need to make sure you're completely stable," Cynthia told her, "but soon."

Remi made a face but didn't complain anymore. She knew she was lucky to be alive, and she wasn't going to protest about that.

April 13, 2020

"So we are seeing a difference?" Midnight clarified as she talked to her chief executives.

"Yes, ma'am, we're not seeing the peak numbers we were concerned with," Marilyn Point told her.

"People are still protesting the Stay at Home Order though," Mark O'Campo, the Commissioner of the California Highway Patrol, told her. "They're out there right now again." He gestured to the front of the Capital building where hundreds chanted various calls to open up the State again.

Midnight shook her head. "People have the right to protest, but they're just going to cause more cases."

The protestors wore no masks and were gathered closely together.

"People not believing in science is the problem," said Gage McGinnis, Midnight's head of the Office of Emergency Services state. "They think they can pray away the virus, or whatever." She rolled her eyes as she shook her head.

"Well, we're just going to have to appeal to their better judgement," Midnight stated.

"Good luck with that," Gage muttered under her breath.

The political divide in the State was only growing as anti-maskers clashed with people doing their best to follow the CDC guidelines. Viral videos of people protesting or having parties while not wearing masks were popping up everywhere. Meanwhile, the President of the United States was continuing to claim that great progress was being made, while also downplaying the need to wear a mask. At the same time, he was urging Governors to reopen their states. Midnight had flatly informed the President that she would open her state when the CDC said it was safe to and not a minute before.

April 20, 2020

"How many more can we get ahold of?" Midnight asked.

"We're doing our best to tap every resource," Gail Weathers, the head of the Department of Education indicated. They were discussing the need for more computers to give to kids who were now distance learning instead of learning in the classroom. "We need more laptops that have built in webcams."

Midnight nodded, her mind racing. "What about parts?"

"Parts ma'am?" Gail queried, unaccustomed to the Governor's rapid thinking and therefore changes in direction in the conversation.

"What if we can get ahold of separate parts, and get people who know how to assemble them?"

"Like who, ma'am?"

"Doesn't the Department of Corrections have a prisoner workforce that works on computers?"

"I… I don't know," Gail stammered.

"Chris," Midnight glanced at her assistant, "can you check with Peterson on that?"

"Absolutely." Chris smiled.

"And see if you can tap Harley and Devin to track down the parts we'd need," Midnight added to Chris' to do list, "we'll pay whatever we have to."

Chris nodded, jotting down more notes.

Gail Weathers stared back at the Governor, still trying to catch up in the conversation. Midnight smiled at the other woman.

"I'll let you know what we find out," Midnight dismissed.

After forty full days in the hospital, Remi was finally released to finish recuperating at home. She was very weak, and still needed a walker to get around, she's lost a total of thirty-five pounds while in the hospital. Her rehabilitation was likely to take months, but at least she was alive, and happy to be so!

BJ arranged to fly them home to Los Angeles in his personal jet a week later. The day they stepped off the plane, California had 33, 862 cases of Coronavirus, there had been 1,223 deaths. Nearly 8,000 of those cases were in Los Angeles County alone, with 617 deaths in their hometown.

"Dye mon, gen mon," Remi commented, as one of the plane's flight attendants pushed her wheelchair up the gang way.

"That's a new one," Wynter said, looking at Quinn and Xandy to see if they'd understood. They both shook their heads. "What's that mean?"

"Beyond the mountains, more mountains," Remi sighed.

It was true, they were returning to a country in disarray. While the US President patted himself on the back and claimed that they had control of the situation, the virus raged with nearly 745,000 cases reported in the United States alone. Alongside that were 41,804 deaths of Americans. The amount was staggering, and it meant that none of them were safe. They were definitely returning to a world changed by this virus.

As the vehicles sent to drive them home, the roads that were usually insane with traffic were eerily quiet.

"When's the last time you saw the 405 this empty?" Quinn commented in an awed tone.

"Never," Wynter replied.

April 23, 2020

Midnight sighed as she set down her cell phone.

"What?" Rick asked.

They were sitting at the table having coffee; Midnight had gotten her daily phone call of the recent COVID numbers.

"125 people died yesterday," Midnight grimaced.

"Jesus..." Rick breathed.

"We're not doing enough," Midnight stated flatly.

"You're doing everything you can," Rick told her.

"We're up to almost 40,000 cases, Rick."

Rick moved to kneel in front of his wife, taking her hands in his. "You're doing everything you can, Midnight," he repeated vehemently, squeezing her hands in his. "You have from the beginning."

Midnight looked down at him, her eyes glazed with tears. "It's not enough." she whispered.

Moving to take her in his arms, Rick knew that he was seeing what no one else was allowed to see. Midnight was rarely vulnerable, or scared, but when she was it was only in front of the people she trusted.

As he held her and stroked her hair, he whispered, "You've got this, babe, we're all with you."

Midnight nodded, against his chest, "I know, I just..."

"You just what?" Rick glanced down at her.

Midnight raised her head, looking up at him. "What if I lose this time?"

Rick shook his head. "Impossible," he told her seriously, "my wife never loses a fight, and she's not going to start now."

Midnight hugged him, knowing that she had to shake off the feeling of panic she was having. The people of the State of California were counting on her, and she couldn't let them down.

Chapter 4

67,816 Cases/ 2,414 Deaths in California
3,580,563 Cases Worldwide/252,886 Deaths

May 1, 2020

"Bring him up on that end," Kai called out, watching as the black Shepherd made his way around the training field.

"Over here." Parker pointed to the area each dog needed to end up in.

"Got it," the officer working with his dog acknowledged.

Parker was enjoying the work, reveling in getting to be outside and working with the K-9s again. Thanks to Kai's pushing, they were working with ten new dogs and officers, putting them through their paces. All officers and staff were wearing masks and practicing social distancing, Kai would accept no less, but at least they were doing work again. It was also a welcome distraction while she anticipated Talon's return.

"She gets in when?" Kai asked, when they took a break later that morning.

"Not till eleven tonight," Parker told her.

"At least she's finally coming home."

"Yep," Parker agreed, "I think she really enjoyed helping out over there though."

"Not exactly the prima donna movie start type, is she?" Kai grinned.

"Talon? Ha! She can be a prima donna one minute, and the hardest working person I've ever met the next," Parker commented, a lopsided smile on her face.

"And you love that about her," Kai's lips quirked in a knowing smirk.

"Damned right." Parker laughed. "This is gonna be a long-ass day."

"Well, I'll keep ya busy till around four, if that helps," Kai offered.

"It does! I appreciate it." Parker clapped Kai on the shoulder. "How'd you get Jericho to go along with this?'

"I told her that we ought to come out of this damned pandemic with some kind of good and that we'd be outside, so less likely to catch anything."

Parker nodded. "Good thinking. It's not like we're in close quarters anyway." She gestured to the open field around them, even as she lifted her coffee to her lips.

"Yeah, Fin says that open air should be generally safe."

"How's she doing with all of this?" Parker canted her head.

"She's stressed," Kai told her honestly. "She's sure this is going to be all bad, and that the government is really downplaying it. They're hearing all kinds of things from other hospitals, running out of respirators, having to pick and choose who has the best chance for survival."

"Damn…" Parker's eyes widened, even as her voice trailed off. "I never thought I'd see something like this in my lifetime."

"Me either." Kai grimaced. "And I'm getting it almost firsthand with Fin coming home every night telling me another story about this patient or that one. She had a mother of five die last week, she couldn't see her kids or her husband before she died."

Parker drew in a deep breath, blowing it out slowly. "Wow, that's awful."

"Yeah, it's really messing with Fin's emotions, I'm not sure how much of this she can take."

"She's used to people dying though," Parker commented.

"Yeah, but those are usually in emergency situations, car accidents, overdoses, falling."

"Appendicitis…" Parker put in, making Kai grin. Everyone knew that was how Kai and Finley had met.

"Yeah, but not stuff like this where people can't be helped. Fin's a surgeon, she wants to fix people, and there's nothing she can fix here." Kai frowned as she shook her head. "It's just really hard on her."

Parker nodded, knowing that she was lucky that she didn't have to hear about the daily tragedies happening in the ER. She just had an adult child that was stressed out all the time about having to go to work and hope she didn't catch it from a customer. Recently Parker had offered her daughter, Kim, the idea of simply taking a leave of absence to stay home with her baby. She was surprised when her daughter didn't jump at the chance to not work. It told her that her own baby was indeed growing up.

At eleven p.m. that night, Parker was waiting at the terminal for private aircraft at LAX. She was alone, the terminal was deserted. After a few minutes she started pacing. She found it amusing that she was so anxious to see her girlfriend again—she was usually a patient person. Talon brought out traits in her that no one ever had before, traits like possessiveness, impatience, and a bigger sense of adventure. Talon Valois was an ever-changing being, not someone that was easily categorized. They'd met during a time when Parker had been on light duty due to an injury; Talon had been determined to get to know the non-effusive K-9 officer, but Parker had been very off-putting. Little by little, Talon had worn her down with not only her constant questions, but also with her kindness and compassion. It had been a disarming combination. Parker had also been confounded by Talon's unpredictable style, one minute she'd be very butch looking with jeans, boots and masculinely cut shirts and jackets, later she'd been very feminine in a dress and heels with makeup and jewelry. Parker never knew who was going to show up.

Ten minutes later, Talon swept through the terminal doors, wearing a flowing dress of teals and blues, with four-inch heels. She was headed straight for Parker. Talon threw her arms around Parker's neck, kissing her ardently as Parker embraced her happily. As their lips parted, Talon buried her face in Parker's neck.

"I missed you so much!" Talon exclaimed.

"I missed you too, honey," Parker told her, setting Talon back on her feet. "Do I need to get the bags?"

"No," Talon said airily, "the guys are already loading it in your trunk."

"You had your keys with you?" Parker asked, surprised.

"You know me, always prepared!" Talon laughed as they turned to walk out of the terminal.

"I have to admit," Parker commented as they walked over to the side lot adjacent to the terminal, "I kind of dig not having to park in the general lot…"

"Aw, getting use to the star stuff, huh?" Talon winked.

"Some parts," Parker scowled as the ever-present Paparazzi started taking pictures.

Talon laughed and waved at the photographers, blowing them kisses as she got into the car as Parker held the door open for her.

"Glad she's back?" one reporter asked.

"No shit," Parker commented, as she rolled her eyes.

Parker drove Talon back to her house—while Talon had never given up her apartment, she stayed with Parker most of the time. Kim was home with her daughter, Ginny, and the two-year-old was thrilled to see Talon. She threw herself at the actress, squealing in delight.

"What is she doing up?" Parker asked. "She was asleep when I left."

"She woke up when your car pulled into the garage," Kim informed her mother.

"Hi babygirl!" Talon enthused, picking up the wriggling child and hugging her close. "How are you?"

"I'm two!" Ginny told her proudly.

"I know, and I'm sorry I missed your birthday last month, but I brought you presents."

"Yay!" Ginna cried happily.

Later, they finally climbed into bed at one a.m.; Parker held Talon close, kissing Talon's neck.

"Mmmm… I'm gonna need more than that," Talon moaned.

"I can definitely oblige," Parker murmured.

Kim made a point of turning up the baby's rain sounds that night to drown out the sounds of their reunion. She was glad Talon was home too.

***

"The death toll is climbing, and these people want the beach reopened!" Midnight growled, as she stood looking out her window at the protestors.

"Seems a bit ridiculous," Joe commented, he'd come to see if there was anything he could do to help.

"It is." Midnight sighed. "I hear Modoc County reopened their churches and businesses."

"Great, their numbers'll only go up now." Joe rolled his eyes.

"I just can't seem to figure out a balance here."

"Midnight, you can't reason with people who don't want to be reasoned with," Joe pointed out, "they don't understand the concept of having what they perceive as their freedom being curbed."

"I'm trying to protect them!" Midnight gestured toward the protestors on the steps below.

Joe shook his head. "And you've always said that sometimes we gotta protect people from themselves sometimes too."

"Damn it," Midnight muttered, her words coming back to haunt her. Joe only grinned in response. He knew he'd made his point.

May 2, 2020

"Harley, where are you going?" Shiloh asked, watching from the couch as her girlfriend walked toward the front door, keys in hand.

"I need to get out of here for a while." Harley sounded agitated.

Shiloh tilted her head, even though it might sound like Harley meant she needed to get away from her; they'd been together constantly since the Stay at Home order, that wasn't what Harley meant. With ADHD to the enth degree, Harley Marie Davidson had a hard time sitting still. Staying in one area, albeit a large home in West Hollywood, was nearly impossible. Harley had used every excuse she could find to leave the house, but Shiloh had clamped down on the impulse when their friends had started getting COVID.

"It's too close to home," Shiloh had told Harley, meaning it figuratively, not necessarily literally.

"I'm not going in anywhere," Harley held her hands up in a quick surrender, "I just need to drive, okay?"

"Please just be careful," Shiloh acquiesced with a sigh.

"Love you!" Harley chimed as she once again headed for the door.

"And leave your notifications off on your phone!" Shiloh yelled after her, just before the door closed. Harley was well known for checking text and email messages while driving, especially if she got a notification of the new message.

Twenty minutes later in her super-charged Stillen 370Z, Harley was amazed at the nearly empty streets. She usually had to deal with traffic to get to the freeway, but not today! As the black sports car climbed the entrance ramp to the freeway, Harley cranked the newest song on her music list, thanks to Memphis. Fort Minor's 'Petrified' pumped from the speakers as Harley sang the rap lyrics, enjoying the taunts asking why everyone was so "petrified" when they arrived on the scene. Harley loved the song, and the ones that followed. Memphis had sent everyone a new playlist, and had, as always, hit the mark with excellent driving songs.

The elation Harley felt when she pressed the gas pedal of her car, feeling it lurch forward with a satisfying growl, was unparalleled. She absolutely loved the feeling of speed, the car moved agilely as she touched the steering wheel to move around a slower vehicle and continuing her drive. It was another hour before she finally turned around to head home, still shocked at how quiet the roads were. This was Los Angeles: the freeways were never quiet!

Regardless, she didn't notice the CHP officer that slid up behind her until he flipped on his lights.

"Son of a…" Harley breathed, even as she signaled to move over, slowing down as she did.

She waited while the officer ran her plates, then rolled down her window to glance up at the officer. He was a younger guy, his mirrored shades giving him that cool, stone-faced façade a lot of cops were known for.

"Good morning officer." Harley smiled brightly, knowing she was caught even as he handed him her license and registration.

"Good morning." The officer smiled too, but it was very definitely a much colder smile. "Do you have any idea how fast you were driving?"

Harley pressed her lips together in circumspect, knowing she'd been really pushing it. "I consider it flying low, rather than driving fast."

The officer nodded his head, his lips pursing his lips in a stern look. Harley could almost feel his eyes narrow behind his shades. Officer Bill Landry had already seen from his search of her plates that she worked for the Department of Justice, so he knew she was a fellow cop. That didn't mean he had to give her a break though.

Leaning down, he took a look in the cabin of the vehicle, then stepped back and looked at the car again. He gave a low whistle; she was definitely a beauty.

"You know how much we could get for this at auction?" he asked, his tone serious.

Harley's eyes widened appropriately. "I, uh," she began, trying to think of a way to placate the officer, realizing she might have been a bit too flip previously. CHP was known to give cops tickets, just because they felt that cops should know better than to drive so unsafely.

Finally, the officer cracked a humorous smile and handed her back her license and registration.

"Just keep it rubber side down, huh?" he told her. "And I dunno, maybe under a hundred?"

Harley laughed, as relief flooded her veins. "Rubber side down, shiny side up," she winked.

"You got it," Officer Landry said, giving her a two fingered salute, "you have a good day."

"You too, sir! Stay safe out there!" Harley called as the officer walked away.

Blowing out her breath as she put her license back in her wallet, Harley knew she'd dodged a bullet. She knew she'd been doing around one-twenty when she'd seen the lights behind her, so the officer was right, he could have impounded her car. The idea that it could be auctioned off wasn't likely, since none of the modifications to her car were illegal, but it would have cost her a lot to get it back. Further, it wouldn't have looked good when it had gotten back to Jericho and Rayden, officers of the law were held to a higher standard to the public even in their personal lives, fair or not.

Half an hour later after getting off the 405 freeway, Harley headed down Wilshire Boulevard. She was intent on getting home, knowing that Shiloh would likely be worried about her. There were few things she worried about in the regular world, but upsetting Shiloh was one of those things. The pandemic had caused her to feel cooped up far too much in the past few months; Shiloh spent a lot of time trying to keep her mind busy, so she didn't go stir crazy, and it was something that Harley realized was a rare thing. Her girlfriend really did understand her like no one else had ever understood her before.

Previously, Harley had experienced a lot of trouble with women, while her good looks and fun personality attracted women in droves, her idiosyncrasies had driven them crazy. Harley Marie Davidson had ADHD, add to that the fact that her profession as a computer programmer, with all the trappings that entailed, and Harley tended to hyper focus on things and forget the world around her. Unfortunately, that included the women in her life fairly often. There had been many fiery, screaming endings to her relationships, many of which had completely blindsided the guiltless and highly preoccupied Harley. Shiloh had been the antidote to those relationships. A previous love interest from high school, Shiloh had been in desperate need of a job at the same time as Harley had needed an assistant and Harley, being the kind, generous person she'd always been, arranged for Shiloh to get the assistant's job.

Shiloh had quickly discovered that her friend from high school had developed not only her computer skills, but also a number of off the wall mannerisms. The highly successful programmer would tend to fade out during high level meetings, choosing to mentally disappear into programmer language and thoughts of ways to solve a problem she was working on for another project. Harley would also forget important meetings and deadlines due to her focus on a certain project, she also had a proclivity for needing to read text messages while driving at breakneck speeds in her Stillen super-charged 370Z, usually scaring the crap out of her passengers. There were plenty of other odd behaviors that made Harley a bit of an odd duck, but Shiloh quickly developed ways of refocusing Harley. She also developed a very definite protective nature over the eccentric self-proclaimed computer nerd.

Harley had never felt more loved or insulated than she did with Shiloh and a deep and sincere love had developed between the two, much to Harley's friends' relief and joy. They'd been together for years now, and Harley had learned to recognize when she was being too distant or was simply worrying or upsetting the love of her life. With that thought in mind, Harley sped down the nearly deserted streets toward West Hollywood and her home with Shiloh. She was just crossing the world-famous Rodeo Drive when she thought that maybe she should pick up some lunch for her and Shiloh, but where? Since the pandemic so many things were either closed or had gone out of business, it was crazy. Harley started scanning the street in front of her for a place to drive through and pick up lunch. She was wondering if Mr. Chow's was doing take out and so barely noticed the black Dodge Ram truck coming down the road on the opposite side. Or the fact that he was weaving slightly in his lane.

Harley was thinking that Shiloh liked the glazed prawns with walnuts when a flash of chrome caught her eye, she realized suddenly that the truck that had been in the opposite lane was now coming straight at her! Harley's mind ran through her options in a fraction of a second and she quickly spun the wheel to the left, putting the passenger side of the Z toward the front so the truck didn't hit her head on, and hoping the side curtain airbag would somehow save her. The impact was explosive as glass shattered all around her. She didn't hear, but felt it as the airbags deployed, even as she was violently thrown into the driver's door. She felt a sharp pain in her head and then everything went black.

She woke coughing as she smelled smoke. Harley had no idea how long she'd been out, but she knew she needed to get out of the car. Reaching for the door handle, even as she unbuckled her seatbelt, she pulled but nothing happened. Her head swimming, she figured that the door was probably jammed. Carefully she did her best to pull herself out through the driver's window, noticing blood coming from a number of cuts on her arms and hands. Gritting her teeth, she ignored the pain in her head and the rest of her body as well. After working herself out of the window, not an easy feat with her long frame, she looked toward the truck. The driver was slumped against the wheel.

Moving to the driver's side, Harley stuck her hand through the shattered window. Feeling for the man's pulse, she didn't feel one.

"Hey! Can you hear me!" Harley yelled at the man. He didn't stir.

Grabbing the handle of the door she pulled at it, it was unlocked, but the door only opened slightly. Bracing her foot against the side of the truck, she put both hands on the handle and used all her strength to pull on the door again, it finally opened with a shriek of metal. Putting her hand in front of his face. She felt for breath and, feeling nothing, she knew she needed to do something. Reaching in, she put her hands under his arms, pulling him out of the vehicle as carefully as she could. Laying him on the ground, she checked for a pulse one more time, but then decided she needed to start CPR. She began doing compressions, and gave a few rescue breaths, feeling lightheaded very quickly but forcing herself to continue. She heard the sirens approaching even as her vision swam, and she wavered. A paramedic ran up as she sat back from a rescue breath, he caught her as she fell backward, passing out cold.

Shiloh picked up her phone, expecting to see Harley's name on the screen, but it was Finley's name instead.

"Hey, Fin, what's up?"

"Shy, I need you to come down to Cedars, there's been an accident," Finley said without preamble.

"Oh my God, is it Harley?" Shiloh stood, grabbing her keys and her purse even as she headed for the front door.

"Yes, she was hit by another car. We're still assessing her condition. I'll hopefully know more when you get here. Drive carefully, I will take care of Harley, you know that."

Shiloh blew her breath, nodding. "I know, I'll be there as soon as I can."

Fifteen minutes later, Shiloh was striding into the emergency room, her mask firmly in place. She spoke to the nurse who started to tell her she needed to go home and wait for a call from the doctor. Fortunately, Jackie recognized Shiloh and pulled her aside.

"I'll handle this," Jackie told the other nurse with authority. "I'll call Fin," she intimated to Shiloh.

"Thank you!" Shiloh whispered fiercely; she'd been ready to do battle with the other nurse. She was damned if she was leaving without an update on Harley's condition.

Finley walked out to meet her a minute later, taking Shiloh's hands in hers.

"Shi, she was in a collision. It would have been a head on, some guy crossed over into her lane, but she was smart and turned the car so he hit on her passenger side." Shiloh blew her breath out slowly to try and calm herself as she nodded. "She has a head injury," Finley continued, "we don't know how severe yet, but she's conscious now and remembers the accident, that's a really good sign."

Shiloh nodded along with what Finley was saying, feeling relief with every word. "Can I see her?"

Behind her mask, Finley grimaced and shook her head, "I wish you could Shi, but they've instituted protocols that doesn't allow visitors in the ER."

Shiloh drew a deep breath, hating this virus even more at that moment. "So what do I do?"

"Will you please trust me to call you?"

"Then why did you have me come down?" Shiloh asked, trying to keep the irritation out of her voice. She wasn't mad at Finley; she was angry that she wasn't able to lay eyes on the woman she loved.

"Well, come right here, and stand by this window. Harley is in this bed here, I'll

open the curtain so you can at least see her and I'll give her my phone, and you can talk to her, okay? But just be quick, I don't want her pushing herself. I'll come back out and talk to you after you two are done."

Shiloh squeezed Finley's hands by way of a thank you. Then Finley went back behind the double doors. She pulled back the curtain and Shiloh saw Harley, as well as the huge bruise on the side of her face.

Shiloh called Finley's phone even as Harley put the phone to her ear.

"Oh babe…" Shiloh breathed, her eyes conveying her dismay.

"I'm okay Shi," Harley told her weakly.

"You don't sound okay."

"I have a vicious headache, but Fin says they can give me something once they establish that there's not need for an operation or anything."

"Do you think brain surgery might help?" Shiloh quipped, her eyes twinkling with humor.

Harley chuckled softly. "You never know."

Behind her mask, Shiloh bit her lips, willing herself not to cry. She didn't want to stress Harley any more than she already was. "I love you, Harl."

"I love you," Harley replied softly, "I'm okay, I promise."

"Then I forgive you."

"But my car…" Harley bemoaned.

"We'll get her fixed, don't worry about that," Shiloh promised.

"Get ahold of Quinn, she'll know what needs to be done," Harley told her.

"Okay… enough about the car…" Finley told Harley sourly. "Tell your girl you love her again, and then you need to rest."

"Yes ma'am," Harley mumbled, lowering her eyes in mock shame. She grinned mischievously as she did, causing Finley to narrow her eyes like a mother would.

"Don't get into trouble!" Shiloh warned. "Fin's my only connection to you!"

Harley pressed her lips together, less than cowed, but knowing that both women were doing their best to keep her spirits up. In truth, Harley was fully aware she could be dead at that moment, so she was grateful to the powers that be that she wasn't.

After they said their goodbyes, Finley walked back outside and talked to Shiloh.

"So once I get all the scans back, I'll call you to let you know what they say. No matter what, I want to keep her for at least tonight and tomorrow so I can make sure there's nothing emergent injury-wise. Okay?"

Shiloh nodded, knowing she was lucky that Finley was their friend. Otherwise, she likely wouldn't get such personalized service. In fact, she'd likely still be sitting out in the waiting room or in her car waiting for someone to let her know what was happening.

"I'm guessing no one knows what happened to her phone," Shiloh commented.

Finley shook her head. "Sorry."

"If I get ahold of it, can I bring it back by for her, so we can talk? You know she'll go nuts if she doesn't have something electronic to play with."

Finley laughed, nodding her head. "Yeah, if you get ahold of it, get it to Jacks she'll make sure Harley gets it."

"Great, thank you so much for this!" Shiloh gave Finley a quick hug, knowing that hugging was frowned upon now, but so overwhelmed with gratitude that she couldn't contain herself.

Finley smiled behind her mask, glad she could be of some help to her friend even in these lousy circumstances.

Later that evening, Jet had pulled some strings with her LAPD contacts and was able to get ahold of Harley's cell phone. Fortunately, the Otter Box case she had her phone in had protected the phone quite well—even when it had gone flying during the accident.

"Apparently it ended up on the pavement," Jet told Shiloh as she handed it to her.

Shiloh closed her eyes, frowning as the image of Harley's phone flying through the air during the collision. It was coupled with images of Harley being thrown around like a ragdoll, which made the image worse.

Jet recognized the look and gave Shiloh and apologetic smile. "Let Harley know we're thinking about her," she offered.

"I will," Shiloh said, hugging Jet, "thank you for getting this back for her, it'll be a lifesaver."

"Happy to do it," Jet told her.

Shiloh was able to drop the phone by the hospital and was pleasantly surprised when Harley called her an hour later. It was good to be connected again, even if it was just through a phone line.

Two days later, Harley was going stir crazy. They'd determined that while her head injury wasn't hazardous to her health, the man she'd given CPR to was very sick with COVID.

"Apparently, the man who hit you had the virus," Finley explained to Harley, with Shiloh on the phone with them.

Harley shook her head. "Might be why he crossed the center divide. And when I did CPR…"

"Yeah, your rescue breaths could have caused transmission to you." Finley nodded.

"Do one good deed…" Harley muttered, knowing that she'd never really had a choice, she couldn't knowingly let a person die without trying to save him.

"So what does this mean?" Shiloh asked, thinking she probably already knew.

"It means I can't release Harley just yet," Finley grimaced. "I know, I'm sorry," she replied in response to Harley's glowering look. "We need to test you, and in the meantime, I'll need to quarantine you."

It wasn't what any of them wanted, but it was a fact. At that point, if Harley was infected and she was sent home, she could give it to Shiloh and Finley wasn't about to let any more of her friends get sick.

Harley and Shiloh were resigned to phone calls every morning and night. Harley had managed to get permission for Shiloh to bring Harley her Alienware laptop, so she at least had something to keep her mind busy with. It didn't take long for her to start feeling like a caged animal without her computer, so Shiloh knew she was doing the hospital staff a favor by reconnecting Harley with her lifeline.

One morning three days later, an extremely weary looking Finley walked Harley's room.

"You don't look like you've gotten much sleep," Harley commented.

"Been up all night," Finley sighed, "I lost another patient this morning."

"Oh shit," Harley winced, "I'm sorry."

Finley shook her head sadly. "Another person who died without even seeing their loved ones again."

Harley swallowed convulsively, thinking that could be her, if she got the virus. It was a sobering thought. She'd never see Shiloh again.

"It's happening a lot?" Harley asked softly.

"Over two thousand in LA alone so far," Finley commented, before stopping to think that she was talking to someone who could possibly have virus. "I'm sorry, Harley, I shouldn't have said it that way," she told the other woman, reaching out to touch her arm.

"No, I understand," Harley said, "I guess it's just something that those of us sitting around the house binge watching shows on Netflix don't even realize. That real people are out here dying without the people they love. It's just too easy to pretend this isn't actually happening, that it's not a movie we're watching. You know?"

Finley drew in a deep breath, tears suddenly glazing her eyes, as the truth hit home. People really didn't understand it from the perspective she lived every day. For her, it was heading into the trenches whenever she was at the hospital, and even being off shift didn't keep her from thinking about people who she'd lost that day. The seventy-five-year-old woman, who'd been so terrified and kept calling for her husband, the thirty-five-year-old man, who had a nasty temperament right up until he realized that he was dying, and cried like a baby while she held his hand as his oxygen levels dropped until he was put into a medically induced coma. A coma he'd never come out of. Every shift it was three, four and five people coding and dying, and there was nothing any of the could do.

Being an ER surgeon usually meant that she wouldn't see this kind of thing—she only dealt with surgery patients. Unfortunately, this pandemic meant it was all hands on deck for medical staff. The overwhelming number of cases just kept growing.

Harley could see by the look on Finley's face that it was taking its toll on the usually vibrant doctor. "I'm so sorry, Fin," Harley said, her eyes misted with tears for her friend. "I wish there was more I could do."

"You just work on getting better," Finley told her.

***

Skyler sat on the back deck tossing the ball for Benny and talking to HQ about their schedule that day. Benny dutifully retrieved the ball, bringing it back and waiting for Skyler to put her hand out palm up, then he'd deposit the ball into her hand so she could throw it again. Skyler and Jams were discussing the training they were doing that day, gearing up for the months to come when things would like ramp up in terms of rescues. Rescues in LA always increased with warm weather; between hikers, beach goers and the California fire season starting earlier and earlier every year, things got busy in a hurry. Skyler smiled when Devin walked outside to sit with her, mug in hand, even as she picked up Benny's ball and lobbed it in Devin's direction.

"I know, we have to make sure that skid has been repaired correctly," Skyler was saying even as Benny came bounding back to her. "Well, we almost lost that basket last time and I'm not taking that chance again…" her voice trailed off as she felt something other than a ball being deposited in her hand. "What the," Skyler began looking down at the stick in her hand. It was a pregnancy test, the word "positive" reading wide and clear. Her light eyes widened as she looked up at her wife, who stood smiling down at her. "Holy fuck!"

Skyler jumped up, hugging Devin and kissing her deeply, even as Jams said, "Hello? Hello? Voodoo?" on his end of the line.

"We're pregnant!" Skyler enjoined, putting the phone up to her ear again.

"Well, it's about damned time!" Jams smiled brightly. "I was beginning to wonder if Sebo was sterile!"

Skyler laughed, knowing that her brother Sebastian, whose friends called him "Sebo," would be sitting right next to Jams, since he'd moved into the apartment he'd previously shared with Skyler.

"Shut da fuck up!" Sebastian cried, laughing even as he did, then leaned in to talk into the phone Jams held. "Congrats sis!"

After she hung up with the boys, Skyler and Devin sat back down.

"Wow…" Skyler mused, "we're finally there."

"Are you scared?" Devin asked.

Skyler contemplated the question for a long moment.

"In a way, yeah."

"Why?" Devin queried, knowing that Skyler had a lot of childhood trauma and realizing that it would definitely affect her wife's thoughts on a child now.

Again, Skyler considered her words, "I guess I worry that the violent streak my father has might be passed on to me."

Devin twitched her lips, always saddened when she thought of the abuse Skyler's father had leveled at her over the years. They'd talked a lot about those incidents over the last couple of years. Skyler had stayed in therapy, after dealing with the PTSD from her time in Iraq and the death of two members of her crew, it had been good for her. Once Devin and Skyler had been started talking about having a baby together, it had become even more important to Skyler to get healthier mentally. They'd started insemination a few months before, using Sebastian's sperm so that the child would truly be a mixture of Skyler and Devin. The doctor had warned it could take a while, but apparently it had only taken five months.

"I think the fact that you've dealt with a lot of that will help," Devin told her wife. "You're aware of your triggers, and I really feel like you've made huge progress with being more open and talking about things that bug you."

Skyler reached up, scratching at the gun shot scar. It was a subconscious gesture, one Devin recognized as a healthy coping mechanism. "Yeah, I think I have. I guess it's just hard to know how I'll handle things with a baby, till we have him."

"Him?" Devin raised an eyebrow. "Why do you assume it'll be a boy?"

Skyler laughed, "I don't know, I guess that's just always what I've pictured when I thought about us having a kid. Is that weird?"

"No," Devin shook her head, "but I'm not sure I want a boy with your good looks running around, we'll have nothing but trouble then."

"Like a female version will be any better?" Skyler quipped.

"True!" Devin exclaimed.

"How are you feeling?"

Devin took a deep cleansing breath, blowing it out. "Excited, scared…"

"Because of my demon child growing in there?" Skyler gestured to Devin's stomach.

Devin shook her head, giving her wife a foul look. "No! I guess because of this crazy pandemic. I've been hearing that women are having to give birth with no family around them. I'm not sure I like that at all."

Skyler chewed on her lip in contemplation, "Well, maybe we could get Fin to do an in-home delivery." She shrugged.

Devin looked a bit horrified by the idea. "With no epidural or anything?"

"Uh, well…" Skyler stammered.

Devin sighed, "I guess we'll figure it out. Right?"

"Exactly!" Skyler agreed.

Later that evening they made a group video chat to tell all their friends about the pregnancy. Once everyone was on (including Harley in the hospital) they made the announcement.

"Oh my gawd, how exciting!" Zoey enthused, many of the others agreed.

"When are you due?" Fadiyah asked.

"Don't know yet," Devin told her, "I really need a doctor to confirm all of this. This could be a premature call."

"Always the cart before the horse…" Jet commented, rolling her eyes.

"Shut up you!" Skyler told her.

"Still, it's awesome news," Jet said, "congrats you two!"

"Cheers!" Quinn added.

"Absolutely!" Jericho nodded.

"I'm very proud," Sebo put in.

"You would be." Jams elbowed him.

"Seriously you two." Skyler shook her head.

It was a brief relief in an otherwise dark time for all of them. They made a point of enjoying it.

***

Harley's test results back and she was positive for the virus. Shiloh did her best not to cry, she didn't want to make things harder on Harley. Regardless, Harley heard it in her love's voice.

"I'll be okay, Shi," she assured. Hearing Harley trying to comfort her, when it was Harley who had the deadly virus, only made it harder for Shiloh not to cry. She sniffled, nodding on her end of the line. "Don't cry, babe…"

"I'm not," Shiloh replied weakly, even as a tear rolled down her cheek.

"Liar." Harley smiled.

"Yeah, so?" Shiloh couldn't help but smile at the accusation as another treacherous tear slipped from her eyes.

They talked for a while longer, and then hung up, promising to talk later in the day.

The room Harley was in was divided by plastic panels and had the capacity for three other people. Within a day of her diagnosis two others were put in her room. One was very sick, and coughed constantly, no matter what the doctor's gave him. Unfortunately, it meant it kept Harley awake at night too. The other person was quite talkative about her condition. She was a younger woman in her mid-twenties, she and Harley talked the first day she was there.

"I was having problems catching my breath, so my doctor decided to admit me." The young woman, whose name was Angie, told Harley who couldn't help but notice that she seemed to preen a bit. Harley imagined that Angie had insisted that she be admitted. "You have the virus too?"

Harley nodded. "Apparently."

"Did it give you that bruise on your face? God, I hope it doesn't cause bruises and stuff!" she exclaimed without waiting for Harley's answer.

"I was in a car accident. I think you're safe."

"You can get it through a car accident?" Angie asked dumbly.

Harley stared back at the younger woman for a long moment, blinking a couple of times, hoping the girl was joking. She wasn't. "Uh, no, I got it from the guy I gave mouth to mouth to."

"Oh, ugh!" Angie made a retching sound. "Why'd you do that!"

Again, Harley paused before answering, thinking that this woman was unreal. "Well, he didn't have a pulse so…"

"And you gave mouth to mouth?" Angie asked, making a face to indicate how disgusting she thought that idea was.

Harley sighed, knowing that she was wasting her breath trying to explain.

"Yeah," Harley answered simply, doing her best not to roll her eyes, as she sat back. It was obvious that the other woman had no concept of doing things for her fellow man.

It didn't make sense to the IT programmer, who immediately took out her laptop and started to work on a program she'd been busy with previously. If Angie noticed the abrupt change in direction from Harley, she didn't mention it.

The following day, the man in their room began suddenly gasping for air and hitting the call button. Harley wanted to do something, but she knew she wasn't allowed to even step out of the room. Instead, she did her best to refocus her mind on her work. Usually, it took no effort at all to focus on numbers and codes, but the nagging thought that she could be like the man in the bed near the door kept presenting itself to her. She did her best to push that fear back down.

Within minutes the medical staff had come into the room and eventually put the man on a respirator. Harley listened to it hiss and click all night that night. She didn't pass on her fear to Shiloh, knowing that it wouldn't do any good to worry her girlfriend any more than she already was.

Finley came by to see her the next day. She stayed far away and kept her mask and face shield on. "How are you feeling?"

Harley shrugged, "Fine, just a bit tired, but I figure that's why." Harley nodded toward the man near the door.

Finley nodded, understanding that the ventilator was a bit noisy. "I can see about moving you."

Harley shook her head, "It's okay, I'll be fine."

Finley nodded, hoping that was true. The last thing she wanted to do was to watch one of her friends die. She knew it was a very real possibility and it terrified her. It was something she talked to Kai about that night.

***

"What if Harley gets bad?" She bemoaned, her head on Kai's shoulder.

"You're doing everything you can, babe," Kai told her, understanding her fiancée's concern, but knowing there was nothing any of them could do at that point. "You said she's doing okay though, right?"

"Yes, I just can't help but think about everyone else I've lost to this thing."

Kai hugged Finley close. "You can't start worrying ahead of time, babe, it'll make you nuts. You just have to take this as it comes."

"I know," Finley exhaled, closing her eyes and doing her best to take in the moment of being close to the woman she loved. She knew that she needed to enjoy the good moments at this point in time and stop borrowing trouble from the future. She also knew it was easier said than done.

"How are things?" Shiloh asked Harley on the phone that same evening.

"Okay, I'm working on that contact program," Harley told her.

Shiloh's lips twitched at her end. She knew Harley was purposefully avoiding talking about how she was feeling and what the state of things were there. She could hear the ventilator in the background and knew that the sound was likely driving Harley crazy.

"Do you want me to bring your sound-canceling headphones down?" Shiloh offered.

Harley smiled at her end: Shiloh always knew what she needed without asking. But then she grimaced as a thought occurred to her. "I'm not sure I want you to keep coming down here, Shi, I don't want you catching this crap."

"I'll be careful, I'll wear my mask and everything," Shiloh assured her, "I know you need to sleep and recharge, Harl, and you can't do that with that noise going on constantly."

Harley's concern warred with her desire to get sleep and also be able to listen to music. Finally, she blew her breath out. "Okay, but only if you're super careful."

"I will be." Shiloh smiled at her end, relieved that Harley was letting her help.

Within an hour, Harley had her headphones and was happily asleep in her bed by the window. She woke late the next morning, feeling better than she had in a while. She worked all day on her program, her head moving to the music on her phone.

"I see you're all set up here," Finley commented that evening when she stopped by, happy to see Harley looking so normal.

"Shi brought me my headphones; it definitely helps," Harley said, gesturing toward the man in the bed.

Finley nodded. "He's not doing well."

Harley grimaced, feeling instantly guilty for thinking the man was inconveniencing her. "Shit, I'm sorry…" her voice trailed off as she tried to search for the right thing to say. "This is just so surreal, it's hard to wrap my head around it. Ya know?" Her voice begged Finley not to think she was a terrible person.

"I do know," Finely answered seriously, "it's okay, Harley. I know this is too far out for most people, but it seems to be the new reality."

"Is it still bad out there?"

"It's just getting worse," Finley told her.

Los Angeles was blowing up with COVID cases, hospitals were running out of room. They were having to repurpose various public facilities. Despite climbing numbers, people were still fighting the wearing of masks. Every day there were new reports of people getting into fights with employees who told them they were required to wear masks inside stores. And still the President heckled people at press conferences for wearing masks. It was nearly unbearable for people like Finley who had to work with patients day in and day out.

***

On Harley's fifth morning in the hospital, she started getting symptoms of COVID. She developed a fever and a cough. Shiloh's stress level went through the roof.

142

"This could be the worst it gets," Finley assured Shiloh.

To make matters worse, the man in Harley's room died that night. Shiloh spent the entire night trying to wrap her head around the possibility that she might lose Harley. It was the longest night of her life.

Fortunately, Shiloh's biggest worries didn't come to pass. While Harley's fever took some time to manage, Finley was able to get it down. The worst of Harley's symptoms abated fairly quickly. It was a relief that Shiloh couldn't begin to describe. The idea of losing Harley just terrified her.

May 18, 2020

"Ready to get out of here?" Finley queried as she walked into Harley's room.

"More than!" Harley commented happily.

Finley smiled, nodding her head, "We'll get you discharged within the hour. Get out of here and stay safe!"

Ten days after coming down with symptoms Harley was completely clear of the virus. Nothing could have made Shiloh happier than to pick up Harley up from the hospital that afternoon. Taking her girl home and getting her settled, was the best feeling in the world. She slept that night with her hand on Harley the entire time, so glad to have her home.

May 19, 2020

"How many?" Midnight asked, her look dumbfounded.

"132, ma'am," Marilyn Point repeated.

Midnight winced, shaking her head. "Jesus…" she muttered, "I thought we were getting ahead of this."

"I'm sorry ma'am, we're doing our best."

"I know," Midnight waved her hand to dismiss Marilyn's apology, "it's not your fault. This is just crazy, and we're still playing catch up."

Marilyn nodded, relieved that she wasn't being blamed. In her experience, it was rare that politicians didn't look for a scape goat.

"Unfortunately, with Memorial Day coming up, we're likely to have a lot more cases," Marilyn pointed out.

***

"I'll go grab the milk while you shop for your veggies." Jericho quirked a grin as she rolled her eyes.

"You won't be saying that tonight when we're having yummy shishkabobs!" Zoey called after her as she strolled through the produce section at Whole Foods.

As she perused the summer squash, she noticed a woman moving toward her. Reaching up, she made sure her mask was secure. She'd be hesitant bringing Jericho with her to the store, she was worried about Jericho's possible exposure to the virus. Jericho already had issues with her lungs due to the damage done years before by a madman's blade. Six months before Jericho had gotten very sick with pneumonia on an ill-fated camping trip and it had made Zoey more cautious with Jericho's health. COVID seemed almost designed to target people with issues with their lungs and Zoey didn't want to take any chances. They'd already canceled their wedding planned for June due to the Stay at Home order in place. Shopping seemed risky to Zoey too, but Jericho was wearing an N95 mask, and making sure to keep her distance from people as best she could. Zoey was doing the same, since the last thing she wanted to do was to catch it and give it to Jericho. Having Harley in the hospital with the virus was bad enough. The group had already dodged bullets with Remi and Memphis, Zoey didn't want to take too many chances.

As she continued down the aisle, Zoey heard raised voices, but did her best to ignore whatever was going on. There always seemed to be an argument going on, so Zoey kept on with her shopping, glancing around to see if Jericho was on her way back yet.

Standing at the bin for onions, Zoey felt someone standing near her. She turned, expecting it to be Jericho, but she was looking up into the unmasked face of a man. He wasn't wearing a mask, and he was wearing a red MAGA hat. Zoey immediately backed up, not taking any chances at that point.

"Where ya going snowflake?" the man sneered.

Zoey was surprised by the vitriol in the man's voice; she'd seen videos online of Trump supporters harassing people wearing masks and practicing social distancing, but she truly never expected to encounter one. At first, she wanted to just ignore him and go on about her business, but her annoyance with him and everyone like him ignoring this pandemic took over.

"To six feet away from you," Zoey replied, her hazel eyes narrowed in irritation.

The man actually took to large steps toward her!

"You sheep just believe anything that shit Governor tells you, don't you?" the man snapped, his grizzled, unshaven face screwed up in antagonistic ire.

"I believe what my friend who's an ER doctor tells me, that people are dying because of this virus, and morons like you are only making it worse!"

The shock played across the man's face in an almost comical way. It was obvious he couldn't believe someone was actually standing up to him, let alone a little slip of a woman like Zoey was. He suddenly realized people were now watching the scene unfold, he looked like a fool at the moment.

Taking a menacing step toward Zoey, he got down in her face. "People die from the flu every year! We don't all have to wear masks and stay home for that! Stupid fucking cunt!"

Zoey felt a shiver of fever run down her spine. She wanted to run away, but she also felt like too many of these Neanderthals had been intimidating people all over the country spouting their leader's ridiculous suppositions.

"We've already surpassed the number of infections in the State that usually the entire country has in flu cases all year long," she told him. She wasn't sure if she was completely accurate, but she also knew that the State was deep in infection rates, and she wanted to shut this guy up.

That brought MAGA hat guy up short for a moment, but since he obviously couldn't argue logic, he resorted to brute force.

"Little cunt," he growled, reaching out. He clearly intended to rip the mask off Zoey's face.

"Touch her and I'll break every bone in your body," Jericho said, standing behind the man, her tone was conversational, , but when he turned to look at her, her face told him that she was very serious.

"What the?" The man's eyes widened as he had to actually look up at Jericho.

Jericho's blue eyes looked past the man to Zoey. "You okay babe?" she asked.

"I'm fine, sweetie." Zoey smiled under her mask, her eyes twinkling. Her knight in shining armor was there now and the man was toast.

The man had recovered from his initial shock as he took in the exchange. "I…you…you're a…" he stammered, as Jericho turned her look back to him.

"Human? Woman? Evolved being?" Jericho supplied.

"Dyke!" the man spat out.

"Aw, there we go." Jericho nodded, having expected that word from the outset. "Yes, I'm a dyke, and I'm a dyke that will take you apart if you don't get away from my girl right now." She leaned in, her eyes narrowing dangerously for emphasis.

The man drew in a sharp breath, sensing the threat easily and obviously trying to evaluate his chances of winning in a fight. To help him make his final decision, Jericho swept her jacket back to reveal her badge clipped to her belt. His eyes went to the badge and widened dramatically; he didn't say another word, simply walking away, accompanied by clapping of some of the bystanders.

Jericho stepped over to Zoey, reaching out to touch Zoey's cheek.

"Are you really okay?" Jericho asked.

Zoey nodded, "I am now. Always my protector."

"And I always will be." Jericho hugged Zoey to her. She'd been blinding mad when she'd seen the man about to accost the woman she loved. "Damned MAGA morons," she muttered.

"I know, so crazy!"

***

"Mom!" Kim called as she walked into the house.

Parker walked out of the kitchen with Ginny in her arms, responding to the stress she heard in Kim's voice. "What's wrong?"

Kim sat down heavily on the couch tears gathering in her eyes. "Someone at work has COVID."

Parker stepped back from the couch immediately, nodding as she did, "Okay, you need to quarantine. When are they going to test you?"

Kim made a sound in the back of her throat, "They aren't, they said I need to go get a test myself."

Parker stared back at her, open-mouthed. "Are you kidding me?"

"I wish I was!" Kim exclaimed.

"Ginny, why don't you make mommy some tea?" Parker set the toddler down in front of her tea set; the child immediately began preparing tea for Kim. "I'm going to call Finley and figure out where you can get tested right away. In the meantime, I'll move

Ginny in with me. You go take a shower and get set up in your room. You can quarantine there…"

Parker's voice trailed off as Kim shook her head, holding up her hand. "Oh, they expect me to still come to work tomorrow."

"And you've now quit that job," Parker said without missing a beat. "Go take a shower."

An hour later, Parker had a test set up for Kim through the clinic at Cedars thanks to Finley. Talon had come home from viewing dailies was ready to storm the store Kim worked at wanting to take the store manage apart for his lack of concern for his employees. "What's wrong with these people!" Talon raged. "They think she's going to come in to see if she can get if she doesn't have it already?"

Parker grinned as she prepared a plate of food to take to Kim, she liked that Talon was protective of Kim too.

"My guess is that they just don't care, or don't believe that COVID is real."

"If I hear one more idiot claim that COVID isn't real, I'm going to lose my shit, seriously!" Talon exclaimed.

"Lose my shit," Ginny repeated.

Parker gave Talon a pointed look.

"Oops, I shouldn't have said that," Talon told Ginny.

"Oops," Ginny repeated with a smile.

Talon picked Ginny up out of her highchair and lifted her up high, "Talon is a bad, bad girl and she should get a spanking."

"Bad girl," Ginny said.

"Needs spanking," Talon prompted.

"Stop it!" Parker laughed, taking the baby from Talon.

149

Talon laughed too. It was good that they could still laugh at this point, and Parker was relieved to have someone to share the situation with. Parker was personally relieved that her daughter wasn't going back to the job that obviously didn't care about their employee's lives, at the same time worried about her possibly having the virus.

May 24, 2020

Cassiana turned over in her bed, looking over at Erin sleeping in the other bed in her dorm room. They'd been essentially living together since early February. It had started as a way to hang out more, but then when the Shelter in Place order had come from the Governor's office, they'd decided to stick together. So far things had been alright.

As Cassiana watched, Erin stirred and opened her eyes. Seeing her girlfriend watching her she smiled.

"You always wake up before me," she commented in mock exasperation.

"I guess I got used to it living with Kai Marou, she's always up early."

"Well, it's gross Cass and you need to stop it," Erin said.

Cass hopped out of bed, leaning down to give Erin a quick kiss on the lips. Cass was always mindful of morning breath and Erin found the concern endlessly amusing. "You want coffee?" Cass asked as she crossed the room.

"Yes, please!" Erin smiled. Even though she was two years older than Cassiana, the younger girl was definitely more dominant in their relationship.

When she'd come to California with her family a few years before, Erin had already suspected that she was a lesbian like her cousin Xandy but being around Quinn Kavanaugh had definitely cemented it. She'd been unable to deny her immediate attraction to the strong, gallant Irishwoman, especially after she'd heard that Quinn had literally lifted part of a house off her baby sister after a tornado had swept through their town. Quinn seemed to epitomize all that was wonderful and fascinating about butch lesbian woman: strong, confident, protective, and very authoritative.

Cassiana's sister Kai Temple was another prime example of those qualities. Even though Cass hadn't lived with Kai most of her life, having come into Kai's life at the age of sixteen when she'd run away from home, she had either learned them from Kai or inherited them in her genes. Erin had already had a number of girlfriends who never even came close to measuring up to the examples of the butches in the group and she'd almost given up when she'd met Cassiana.

Three years before

"Erin, can you get the door?" Xandy called, as she continued to hold the shelf Quinn was putting up for her in the bathroom.

"Sure," Erin got up from the couch to answer the door. There stood Kai Temple and a younger woman with her. "Hi Kai, come on in."

"Erin, this is my little sister, Cassiana," Kai introduced.

Erin nodded at the other girl. "Hi Cassiana, nice to meet you."

"Hi, call me Cass," she said, a sparkle in her eye. As their eyes met and held for an extra second, Erin immediately realized that this girl was likely a lesbian too.

"Cass..." Erin repeated with a smile, but then she realized Kai was looking at her expectantly and moved out of the doorway to let them in. "Kai, Quinn and Xandy are in the master bathroom." She gestured toward the back of the house.

Kai nodded. "Thanks," she said, and headed off on that direction.

Erin and Cass regarded each other for a long moment.

"Um, do you want something to drink?" Erin finally offered, realizing that she was just standing there.

"Sure," Cass replied, trying to be smooth.

Erin led the way to the kitchen, surprised at how completely awkward she felt suddenly. Opening the fridge, Erin pointed out the different options.

"Pepsi works," Cass said, smiling.

Erin reached in grabbing two sodas but then fumbled them when she went to close the refrigerator. Cass caught one before it hit the floor and Erin went for the other, but missed it, the can bounced on the floor and then began spinning and spraying its contents all over the floor.

"Aaa!" Erin exclaimed, reaching for a towel as Cass grabbed at the can, running it over to the sink. Unfortunately, Cass also stepped in soda and slipped landing on the floor with a yelp.

"Man down," Cass croaked, feeling like a big dork at that moment.

Erin stared down at the younger girl and couldn't stop the giggle that bubbled up, she immediately clapped her hand over her mouth, but Cass was grinning by that time. Within moments they were both laughing hysterically as Erin helped Cass up off the floor. They were friends instantly.

After their coffee, Erin and Cassiana started on schoolwork, taking a break at lunch to watch the news. Midnight Chevalier had taken to doing a daily check-in on the Coronavirus pandemic. That afternoon she reported that there were currently 110,549 cases of COVID reported in California, and that there had been 3,984 deaths due to the virus. She went on to talk about the need to stay safe, to wear a mask and to avoid gatherings.

"Almost four thousand people..." Cassiana shook her head.

"That's crazy!" Erin exclaimed, unable to fully believe what was happening.

Later that day, the evening news talked about the Republican party having filed a lawsuit against the Governor. The lawsuit protested the executive order to send out mail-in ballots to all Californians for the election happening in November They also reported on a protest about the Shelter in Place order.

"Idiots!" Cass raged. "They're going to get everyone else sick with their stupid bullshit."

Erin simply shook her head sadly. Things were getting scary.

That night when they went to bed, they each climbed into the twin sized beds in the room they shared. Before long, however, after much tossing and turning, Erin got out of her bed and moved to crawl in with Cass, who obliged her by moving to the very edge of the bed.

"Can't sleep?" Cass asked.

Erin shook her head, snuggling a little closer to her girlfriend. "I can't stop freaking out about this whole thing." Turning her face up to look at Cass, she said, "What if this is the beginning of the end of the world?"

Cassiana hugged Erin closer, kissing her forehead, "I'm sure it's not, but it is definitely something I don't think has been seen in a long time. We'll get through this babe, we just have to be careful."

Erin nodded, not completely convinced, but taking comfort in Cass' confidence.

The next morning, they rearranged the dorm room, pushing the two twin beds together. Erin ordered them a larger mattress on Amazon Prime. Luckily it arrived two days later, but not before Cassiana, who gallantly slept on "the crack", ended up on the floor.

"Man down, man down!" she called out, laughing all the while.

Erin decided that if she had to be stuck with anyone during a pandemic, she was definitely glad it was Cassiana Temple.

Chapter 5

423,932 Cases/ 8,142 Deaths in California
13,899,939 Cases Worldwide/656,802 Deaths

July 14, 2020

"Come right, ten," Jams told Skyler. "Back easy…"

"Roger that. Just keep an eye on that fire," Skyler breathed into her mic, "I don't need our ass catching."

Jams grinned, he knew she was serious, but the idea was simply insane. The Lake fire had only been burning for a couple of days, yet it had already burned many thousands of acres of land, and destroyed multiple structures. LA Fire and Rescue had been called in to rescue some campers at the far end of Hughes Lake. The campers had hiked up a nearby hillside to "scout the area" according to the report they'd received from dispatch. Skyler and Jams had rolled their eyes at that account. People were forever trying to outsmart natural disasters and it rarely worked out well for them. Such was the case here.

"You got 'em?" Skyler called back to her crew members.

"Yeah, we see 'em," Tom called back, "basket deploying."

"Got it," Skyler replied, "hold her steady, Jams."

Ten minutes later they had all four members of the family onboard. They looked dirty and a bit banged up, but fortunately none of them had been burned. Unfortunately, there was still a definite problem. The father, a man of about forty-five, was coughing and feverish, and none of the family was wearing masks.

"Sir, how long have you had a fever?" Tom asked the man, as he glanced at Jerry, even as he himself adjusted his mask.

The man waved his hand dismissively. "Don't start this Coronavirus crap with me," he practically snapped, "I don't believe any of that snowflake shit."

In the cockpit, Skyler glanced over at Jams, "What did he just say?"

"Apparently he doesn't believe in the virus," Jams curled up his lips at the sheer stupidity of the man's statement.

Skyler keyed her mic. "You get masks on those people now," she told Tom in no uncertain terms.

"Probably too late," Tom replied under his breath, even as he reached for a box of paper masks, handing one to each of the kids and the wife.

"No," the man shook his head, putting his hand out to block his kids from putting the masks on, "we're not doing that shit."

Skyler leaned around the rear seat in the cockpit. "Sir, you and your family are wearing a mask as long as you're on my helo."

"You can't tell me what to do!" The man huffed. "You're trying to violate my civil rights."

"And you're endangering my crew with your ignorance!" Skyler called back. "Put the masks on or get off my ride!"

"You can't kick me off, my tax dollars pay your salary and for this helicopter!"

"You wanna bet me?" Skyler growled.

"He does realize we pay taxes too, right?" Tom quipped, raising an eyebrow at Jerry.

"Guessing he doesn't," Jerry replied.

"John, maybe we should just—" the man's wife began, but he cut her off.

"Shut up Joanie!" he snapped. "I'll have your license for this!" he yelled in the direction of the cockpit.

"Maybe you'd like it back out on that ridge?" Skyler countered.

"Fucking snowflake cunt!" the man swore.

"Sir, either calm down, or we'll have to restrain you," Tom told the man, his tone serious.

"I have rights!"

"You are also required to follow our directions on board our aircraft," Jams called back to the man, "so either follow our directions, or you'll be cuffed and gagged."

"You can't do that!" The man insisted vehemently.

"Wanna try us?" Jerry asked, flexing the muscles that were evident—even in the uniform he wore.

The man eyed Tom and Jerry, who both spent many hours a week in the gym. He decided he'd better cooperate at that point.

Back at the station an hour later, Skyler was on the phone with Devin.

"So thanks to asshole, I'll need to quarantine for the next two weeks."

"Awww, can you at least do that here?" Devin asked, gesturing around her to their house in Malibu.

"No, I'm not taking any chances right now," Skyler told her.

157

Devin sighed; she'd already known the answer before she'd heard it. Skyler was being extra cautious at this point. She put her hand to her still flat stomach. They'd found out she was eight weeks pregnant the week before. They were both thrilled, but also a bit concerned with the ever-worsening pandemic.

"I guess there's nothing we can do, huh?" Devin worried.

"No," Skyler told her, "we just have to hope that Mr. Trumpanzee didn't infect my whole crew."

Devin couldn't help but smile at the label Skyler gave the obvious Trump supporter, it was growing ever clearer who the virus deniers in the country were. With a President that had recently told people that wearing masks was a bad idea, the divide between people who believed in science and doctors and people who didn't was only growing.

"So I'm not going to see you for two weeks?"

"Sorry babe," Skyler grimaced, it wasn't the first time she'd had to quarantine in the last four months. They frequently had people they rescued who'd showed symptoms to the point where Skyler hadn't felt safe being around Devin, but she'd usually quarantined at home in a separate room. "I don't want to take chances with your pregnancy... you understand right?"

"Of course I do," Devin assured her. "Geeze, between Fin, Fadi and River, this group is fully saturated on the dangers of this virus. Trust me, I get it. It doesn't make it suck less though."

"I know, but we can video chat every night, okay?"

"Okay," Devin agreed. "Of course, the chances are you'll be working like crazy with this damned fire season firing off like it is."

"Tell me about it!" Skyler grouched. "It's frigging crazy out there already. Hey, so I'll have Sebo drop by the house to pick up a bag if you'll pack one for me."

"You know I will," Devin told her. "I love you, stay safe the rest of your shift, okay?"

"I will. Love you."

July 16, 2020

"So yeah," Skyler settled her iPad on her chest as she video chatted with Devin, "that John guy from yesterday has COVID."

Devin paled slightly. "Oh God…" she breathed.

"It doesn't mean we'll get it babe," Skyler told her.

"But you could."

"Yeah, we could, but I really didn't come in contact with him, neither did Jams."

"But Tom and Jerry did," Devin reminded her.

"I know," Skyler grimaced, "we just have to wait and see."

"That sucks," Devin sighed, "I wish you could sue that asshole."

Skyler chuffed, screwing her lips up in a sneer, "Yeah, you and me both. I'm so sick of these idiots who don't want to believe in what the doctors are saying."

"I know, they had some idiot on the news earlier claiming that this is just some scheme thought up by hospitals to make extra money." Devin rolled her eyes, shaking her head.

"Hell in a fucking handbasket," Skyler muttered.

"And fast!" Devin countered. They were both silent for a long few moments.

"So how's my baby?" Skyler changed the subject with a grin, not wanting to discuss the state of the world anymore. "I'm fine, thanks for asking." Devin's eyes sparkled with humor.

Skyler laughed, "I meant the little pea pod."

"I know what you meant, ya brat," Devin narrowed her eyes at her wife, "the pea pod is making me wanna throw up regularly."

"Ugh," Skyler frowned, "did you talk to Savannah about what to do about that?"

"She suggested the Saltine route, but Fin said I'd be better off sucking on ginger mints, Shenin agreed. They do seem to help some."

"How long does this part last?"

"First trimester, hopefully," Devin held up crossed fingers, "so maybe a couple more weeks."

"Less barfy would be good." Skyler stifled a yawn.

"How long did you work today?"

"We pulled a fourteen-hour shift."

"But if you're supposed to be quarantining..." Devin pointed out.

"We wore our oxygen masks, so we couldn't infect anyone if we have it."

"That's not fair," Devin said, "other people get to stay home and quarantine, you guys have to work."

Skyler shrugged. "What else am I going to do for fourteen days? Besides, you know how it is. They need us right now, as long as we're not showing any symptoms and we're safe, it'll be okay. These fires aren't helping."

Devin sighed, "I know, that's what I get for marrying a first responder."

"Yes ma'am."

July 18, 2020

"Well, Tom and Jerry got it," was the first thing Skyler told Devin two days later.

"Damn..." Devin breathed. "Are they doing okay?"

"So far, so good, just fevers and body aches. They're sending me new guys."

"How's that going to go over?"

"It'll be okay," Skyler told her, "we train using the same terminology, so that we're able to swap teams and team members without any communication issues."

Devin drew in a deep breath, nodding as she blew it out. "I miss you."

"Miss you too, babe." Skyler smiled softly.

"Are you feeling okay?"

"I'm fine, just bored when I'm not in the air," Skyler told her.

"I know," Devin widened her eyes at her wife, "how many hours today?"

"Same, fourteen," Skyler said.

"Well they're definitely getting their money's worth!"

Skyler chuckled. "Speaking of which, how's that new program going?"

"Slow, but sure." Devin rolled her eyes. "I swear I'm already experiencing that baby brain drain they talk about."

"Oh great, I'm sure the company that hired you will be happy to hear about that."

"Shut up, you," Devin told her, giving her a narrowed look.

Skyler only laughed, Devin at half speed was still better than most programmers in her field.

***

That same day, the United States' death toll from Coronavirus surpassed 140,000 dead. The next day President Trump was quoted as saying, "I think we have one of the lowest mortality rates in the world."

"The guy is off his fucking rocker," Midnight muttered, she'd been in her office for hours already, having left the night before at eleven p.m., and returning the next morning at six a.m.. "What are our numbers?" she asked Chris, who was also in the office early that morning.

Chris checked her screen, pulling up the appropriate documents. "We're at nine thousand and twenty-six."

Midnight blew her breath out slowly, feeling absolutely sick. "Christ, are we getting anywhere?"

Chris pressed her lips together, knowing it wasn't an actual question and wishing she could have better news.

July 24, 2020

"I'm sorry, ma'am, but as you know we've got multiple fires going off everywhere!" Gage practically shouted over the rotor blades of the OES helicopter she was in. "I'm headed up to Lassen to see where we are."

"I understand," Midnight replied, knowing it had been a long shot to get help from her office of emergency services.

"Looks like this is going to be a crazy year all the way around," Gage commented.

"You're telling me," Midnight agreed. "Be safe."

"Thanks boss!"

Midnight hung up the phone, glancing at Chris, her assistant.

"Nope," she told the girl, "keep calling around, we're going to need to get some more support for the hospitals. We're headed to the airport to head up to LA for a scouting trip. We gotta find some more space for hospital beds."

Chris nodded grimly, knowing that the pandemic was only worsening. It was taking its toll on all of their resources.

July 27, 2020

As Catalina made her way through the big box store she'd ventured to in order to find some of the items she and Jovina needed, she heard a loud scream. The cop in her kicked in instantly: leaving her cart she moved through the aisle, headed in the direction the scream had come from. As she rounded the corner, she was surprised to see a large man standing over a much smaller, older woman.

"You should've just moved!" he was yelling.

"I didn't see you," the woman offered feebly.

Cat moved to help the woman up as others stood by gaping at the scene. The woman smiled graciously at Cat and got unsteadily to her feet. Leaning down, Cat picked up the package of toilet paper laying on the ground—but the man was doing the same.

"That's mine!" the man yelled as Cat grabbed it first.

Glancing at the lady she'd just helped up, Catalina asked gently, "Was this yours?"

"I said it's mine!" the man repeated, reaching for the package with his large, meaty hand.

Turning, Cat kept it away from him. She gave the older lady a pointed look. "Did you have this?"

The lady nodded, her blue eyes wide with obvious fear. With that, Cat dropped it in the woman's basket. The man immediately moved to reach for the package again. Cat moved to stand in front of the basket as well as the poor woman the man was bullying.

"Bitch!" the man snapped, reaching out to shove Cat aside.

To his surprise Cat reacted by grabbing his wrist and, using his forward momentum, she spun him around with his arm up behind his back. Something she'd done a million times as a police officer. As he howled in both anger and pain, Cat glanced behind her at the lady.

"Just go ma'am, I'll take care of this guy."

"Tha-thank you." The woman's eyes were now shining with both appreciation and surprise.

Cat smiled back at the woman, but since she was wearing a mask it simply showed in her eyes. As the woman walked away pushing her cart, Cat turned her attention back to the man she was holding.

"Let's go," she said to him, "I'm sure security would like a word with a guy who roughs up old ladies over toilet paper."

"Who the fuck do you think you are!" The man tensed as he started to turn on Cat, but she held him fast.

"I think I'm a cop who just overheard you verbally, if not physically, assaulting an elderly woman," Cat informed him as she marched him through the store, his arm still immobilized behind his back.

At one point she could feel him tensing. Everyone in the store was stopping to watch the spectacle they made: this petite blond marching a man at least a foot taller than her down the main aisle of the store.

"Don't try it," Cat cautioned him, "I may seem small, but I've beaten bigger and badder than you and come out on top." The supreme confidence in her voice made him think twice.

"Are you louca?" Jovina asked her when she related the incident later at home.

Cat chuckled, loving that Jovina likely didn't even realize how often she slipped into Portuguese with her. "No babe, I'm not crazy, but I'm not going to let some guy badger a poor little old later so he can wipe his ass fifty times a day."

"These people are insano about toilet paper!" Jovena threw her hands up, shaking her head.

"Yeah, it's pretty nuts out there." Cat nodded as she put the items she'd bought wherever they'd fit in their cabinets. "But I was able to score some beans and rice and even some chicken so we should be good for a while."

"So you know people are nuts, but you step into a fight with some bear of a man?"

"Babe, you know I can handle myself," Cat gave her girlfriend a wicked grin, "and if I start to lose, I always have back-up." She pulled the handgun from the holster at the small of her back. "I'm always safe."

Jovina pressed her lips together, still not liking that the woman she loved put herself in unnecessary danger.

"Jovi, what was I supposed to do? Let him beat up an old lady?"

Jovina sighed, shaking her head. "No, I know the champion in you wouldn't allow that."

Cat moved to take Jovina in her arms, smiling as she did. "So stop giving me a hard time then."

"Pirralho," Jovina muttered, calling Cat a brat.

"And you love me."

"True, but that doesn't make you any less annoying." Jovina smiled, even as Cat nuzzled her neck.

July 30, 2020

Skyler arrived home, having never gotten any symptoms, much to Devin's relief. Devin waited patiently for Skyler to take a shower, to make sure she was completely safe to be around her wife and their baby. Once her shower was done, however, Devin showed her how much she'd missed her. It was good to be home.

***

Finley walked into the hospital exam room and was only mildly surprised to see that the man waiting there wasn't wearing a mask. He had one, but it was pulled down around his chin. Picking up his chart, Finley silently regretted not searching longer for a pair of goggles and a clear face shield. Supplies were once again running low at the hospital, and all she'd been able to do was don two paper masks before entering this hospital room.

"Sir," she sighed, as she saw that he had all the classic symptoms of Coronavirus, "you need to put that mask on your face, please."

"It's on my face," the man stated, his sneer already nasty.

"I mean over your nose and mouth," Finley informed him, keeping her distance until he did as she said.

"The President said this thing is going away."

"Your President in wrong." Finley replied sharply. She'd lost more patients the night before to the virus and was in no mood to hear what the "President" thought. "Now, put your mask on, or I'm leaving the room."

"He's your President too!" the man barked angrily.

"Like Hell he is!" Finley barked back, turning to leave the room. Obviously, the man couldn't be reasoned with and she intended to call security.

Before she could get the door open, however, the man suddenly had his arm around her shoulder, yanking her back against him. "He's your fucking president too, you stupid fucking sheep!!"

Finley did her best to keep her face turned away from him, but he was yelling at that point, his spittle going everywhere. Instead of struggling against his hold, Finley did as she'd been taught by Kai: she relaxed, making him think she was accepting what he was saying and doing. He, in turn, loosened his hold on her. She promptly stomped down on his instep while elbowing him in the stomach at the same time. His surprise caused him to let go of her, and she was able to get out of the room as quickly as possible.

Outside the room, she yelled for security. She then headed to the eyewash station in the next empty room, doing her best to wash off any trace of the man's spit from her face and eyes.

"What happened?" Jackie asked as she walked in.

"Get back Jax!" Finley warned. "This guy who likely has the virus, just attacked me and he wasn't wearing his mask!"

"Oh lordy, people do be crazy right now!" Jackie shook her head, rolling her eyes heavenward.

"Another damned Trumper, who thinks whatever that idiot says is gospel. I swear to all that is holy, that man will be the death of this country!" Finley raged.

Just then, Mark Davis, the resident in charge walked in.

"What happened?" he asked, his brows knit with worry.

Finely took a deep breath, blowing it out slowly through her nose before speaking.

"A patient with COVID symptoms and no mask grabbed me."

"Are you alright?" he asked, his eyes scanning her for signs of injury.

"I'm fine," Finley forced a grin, "being engaged to a physical trainer comes in handy when she's taught you self-defense."

To Finley's surprise the normally very serious Dr. Davis chuckled.

"Good for you! I want you to go home and quarantine, I'll personally test this man and let you know when we get the results."

"I'm gonna call Kai and have her come get you," Jackie put in.

"No, I'll get home on my own, I'd rather be in my own vehicle if I'm contagious."

Jackie didn't like that answer but shrugged, she wasn't going to argue.

Half an hour later, Finley was in her shower in the new bathroom just off the garage. Kai wasn't home—she'd left a note on the inside of the bathroom door saying she'd be back, that she'd gone to get supplies for them, Cass and Erin. After a thorough hot shower, Finley, wearing a mask and gloves, grabbed a few things out of the bedroom she shared with Kai, and moved herself into the guest bedroom at the opposite side of the house. She texted Kai about what had happened, telling her that she'd moved into the guest bedroom. Kai's reply was simple.

We'll talk when I get home.

A couple of hours later, Finley heard the light knock on the guest bedroom door. Getting up she went to the door, pulling on her double mask as she did.

"Don't come in, Kai," Finley said as she heard the doorknob jiggle.

"You locked it?" Kai sounded offended.

"I'm sorry babe, I don't want to expose you in case the guy was positive."

She heard Kai's grunt of annoyance. "What the hell is wrong with people! I hope someone beat the living crap out of the guy."

169

On her side of the door, Finley grinned, "I'm sure security wasn't gentle with him, if that helps."

"It does," Kai answered. There was a long pause. "What can I do Fin?"

Finley grimaced, knowing it was Kai's nature to fix things. "Nothing babe, I've got what I need in here."

"Did you eat yet?"

"No," Finley answered.

"How about a nice fresh Chinese chicken salad?" Kai replied, a smile in her voice.

"Sounds yummy, thank you."

An hour later, Kai knocked on the door to the guest bedroom and set down the tray of food. She had located a rose in the backyard to put alongside the meal, along with utensils and a drink. She dutifully back away from the door to let Finley come out and retrieve the tray.

"Aw, Kai…" Finley mused when she saw the rose. "Thank you."

Kai inclined her head. She was wearing a mask, but Finley could see the smile light her eyes. "Can we have dinner together?" Kai asked, gesturing to the door.

"How…" Finley asked.

Kai made the motion of Finley closing the door, and said, "I'll sit here, you sit on the other side."

Finley laughed softly. "Well, this'll be an odd date."

"Best we can do under the circumstances."

"True." Finley nodded, and softly closed the door, then moved to sit down facing the door.

Once Finley was safely back in the bedroom with the door closed, Kai grabbed her plate and glass of water and sat down next to the door on her side.

"So, other than the crazy ass that tried to give you COVID, how was your day?" Kai asked.

Finley laughed out loud, and then proceeded to talk about her day. Kai did the same. It was the first of many meals they would share that way.

Two days later they found out that the man had indeed been positive for COVID. Finley did a test on herself, and Kai took it to the hospital. Jackie came outside to retrieve it.

"How's our girl doing?" Jackie asked.

"As well as I think can be expected. No symptoms yet though, so let's hope she didn't get it."

"I'm praying!" Jackie exclaimed. "You take good care of her, ya hear?"

"I will, I promise."

Jackie put her hand on Kai's arm, "I know, baby, you always take care of her, that's why I love you so much!"

Kai chuckled. Jackie had always been her biggest proponent, which she'd always appreciated. "You take good care too, Jax."

"Oh I'm being super careful, don't want to bring this mess home to my family either!"

"Good." Kai nodded, her tone serious. Finley had made sure Kai knew exactly how deadly this virus was, she didn't want anyone taking chances.

Two days later, the results of Finley's test came back. She was positive for COVID. Kai was beside herself with worry. Finley assured her that it wasn't necessarily bad, that others had gotten the illness, but never got terribly sick.

"That better be the version you have, or I'm hunting that bastard down and killing him." Kai commented darkly.

They found out later that week that Kai wouldn't have had far to go, the man and his entire family had ended up with COVID. Jackie kept them updated. He was in the ER by the end of the week, and on a ventilator shortly thereafter. Again, Finley had to talk Kai down off the worry ledge.

"It doesn't mean I'm going to get really sick," she reasoned with Kai through the bedroom door. "I've only got cold symptoms at this point. It could be that it never amounts to more than that. Just breathe babe."

Kai leaned her forehead against the door, doing her best to listen to what Finley was saying and not worry even more. It was definitely a trying time.

August 1, 2020

"You're in contact with Hunter and Kori at Cal Fire, right?" Gage queried.

"Good morning, Jock, and how are you doing?" Gun grinned as she leaned back in her chair.

Gage laughed at her end, shaking her head. "Sorry, Gun, my brain has been running in every direction today. We're good down here, how are you?"

"Yes, I'm sending resources Cal Fire's way, Hunter and I talk most mornings at this point. With that damned Caldwell fire merging with Gillem day before yesterday they're up over eighty thousand burned now. This is a shit season all around!"

"We're up over two hundred thousand burned already, and we're just getting started!" Gage intoned.

"Shit season," Gun repeated dismally.

"And how are you?" Gage prompted with curled lips.

"Fuck you Jock." Gun laughed.

"Is Sable back in the country?"

"Yeah, she's back, Scotland was going nuts with their government not really doing a lot, but she was able to get out since what restrictions they did have were easing up."

"Good." Gage sighed, "Things here are good, Caitlyn is already sick of distance learning."

"Aren't all the kids at this point?"

"True, but Kit's been trying to make it fun. We're watching to see what happens with school opening back up or not."

"Deaths are going up," Gun commented.

"Infections are falling though," Gage offered hopefully.

"I hope you two aren't holding your breath."

"We're not."

August 2, 2020

Zoey poked her head into Jericho's home office.

"What do you want for lunch?"

Jericho looked up from the report she was reading, smiling. This had become a routine for them. They were both working from home, each in their respective home offices, the ones Jericho had set up when they'd gone to telecommute only during the pandemic. Zoey regularly asked what she wanted for breakfast and lunch. In truth, it was nice to be able to eat together and see each other off and on all day long.

"What are my options?"

"Leftovers from last night's dinner, or a sandwich."

"Leftovers works."

"Got it," Zoey replied, simply. Jericho stared after her fiancée as she left to fix lunch. She sensed something wasn't right. Her suspicions only deepened when Zoey was unusually quiet during lunch.

"Everything okay?" Jericho asked as she picked up their plates from lunch to take them to the sink to rinse them.

"Yes," Zoey answered simply.

At the sink Jericho frowned but decided to chalk it up to Zoey being busy with a project. Zoey had started working as the head of California for All Women, having been appointed by Midnight. The program was about promoting women's ability to work and thrive in the State of California. There were many moving parts to the program and Zoey had still been wrapping her head around it when COVID had hit and caused everyone to work remotely.

Now Zoey was working on a project to increase women being hired or appointed to management positions within the State. Meetings had been pushed from in-person to online, which meant more organizing and ensuring that technical issues could be worked out. It was a constant work in progress and was causing Zoey more than a little stress.

Later that evening, Zoey had decided to take a bath. It was a chilly night, so it seemed like a perfect chance to utilize the soaking tub Jericho had installed in the master bathroom. One of the many projects Jericho had taken on since being home so much. A few minutes later, Jericho looked in on the younger woman. She couldn't help but grin at the way Zoey lay in the tub with bubbles covering her as the tub continued to fill.

Zoey caught Jericho's grin and laughed. "It keeps me warm!"

"I'm sorry?"

"Having the bubbles covering me keeps me warm while the water fills up the tub."

Jericho looked skeptical but nodded all the same.

"It does!"

"Yes dear," Jericho responded dutifully.

"Stop it," Zoey answered.

Jericho considered her fiancée for a long moment, noting that Zoey once again seemed a bit melancholy.

"So what's going on babe?" Jericho queried, while leaning against the doorjamb.

Zoey glanced over, then shrugged. "Nothing really."

Jericho frowned, moving to sit on the floor next to the tub. She pushed her long dark hair back behind her ears—a sign she was digging into a problem. Zoey sighed, knowing she wasn't being very convincing with her denial that anything was wrong.

"Come on, out with it."

Zoey twitched her lips, really not wanting to talk about the thoughts swirling around in her head. She shrugged again, hoping

Jericho would just give up. She knew better, Jericho Tehrani was far from affable when it came to Zoey's problems.

"It's stupid." Zoey shook her head.

"Then it should be easy to solve." Jericho smiled, her light blue eyes sparkling humorously.

Zoey pressed her lips together, smiling despite obstinacy. Jericho always had a way of making her feel better, no matter what was happening. "It's not really something that needs to be solved."

Jericho sighed. "Don't make me climb in there with you…"

"You have your new slippers on, you'd ruin them."

Jericho pursed her lips, knowing that Zoey was just being difficult, but determined all the same. "Then you'd just have to buy me another pair."

"Those are a hundred-dollar deerskin slippers!" Zoey exclaimed as Jericho stood up and lifted a slippered foot. "Don't you dare!"

Jericho laughed, sitting back down. "Then spill it."

"I just…" Zoey began, but shook her head, looking away.

Jericho canted her head. "Does it have to do with the wedding?"

"It's stupid," she insisted angrily, "people are dying! And I'm being a baby about a wedding."

"So what are you thinking?" Jericho asked carefully.

Zoey glanced over at Jericho sharply, then forced herself to replay how Jericho had just asked the question. There hadn't been any kind of attitude, it was a simple question. The fact was that the topic was so sensitive at this point, that Zoey knew she was hearing rudeness where there wasn't any, and she knew she needed to stop.

The pandemic had blown apart their wedding plans to marry in South Lake Tahoe on June fourteenth. They'd been in lockdown on that date but had already canceled so they didn't lose the money Jericho had paid for the Diamond Package wedding. At the time it had broken Zoey's heart to cancel, but she'd understood it was the only thing they could do.

There'd been many discussions about what they should do, should they reschedule? Should they wait until things calmed down? Should they just go down to the courthouse and do a civil ceremony? Was the courthouse even doing marriages? It was frustrating!

"Zoe?" Jericho queried, seeing that her fiancée was busy being in her head.

Zoey sighed, "I'm sorry, I was talking myself down."

Jericho raised an eyebrow in response and Zoey blew her breath out.

"I'm just trying not to go crazy with this whole thing."

"The pandemic or the wedding?" Jericho grinned.

"Both!" Zoey laughed.

"Well, what's most important to you at this point in time?" Jericho asked, trying to get to the heart of the matter.

"That you belong to me."

"I already belong to you," Jericho told her.

"I mean, legally, damn it," Zoey laughed.

"Okay, so let's call the courthouse and see if they're doing ceremonies at this point."

"But your parents… our friends…"

"We can have a party later, babe, we could even do the ceremony again," Jericho offered.

"Really? That would be okay with you?" Zoey asked wondrously.

Jericho shrugged. "The legalities are the boring part, babe. It's the party people come for."

Zoey bit her lip, her eyes sparkling. "Then that's what we should do."

"Alright, then that's what we'll do."

They found out the next day that they would do a wedding, but only remotely.

Jericho shook her head, "I have a better idea."

"Like what?" Zoey asked.

"You'll see." Jericho smiled.

Three days later Zoey received a handwritten note from her wife, left on her pillow first thing in the morning. It read: "Be in your best dress and meet me in the back yard tonight at eight." She was even more surprised when the doorbell rang an hour later; when she opened it, she found Xandy, Jazmine and Natalia, all masked up and holding various bags.

"We've come to pamper you!" Xandy said. "We've all been stuck inside for weeks, haven't seen anyone or been anywhere, so we're safe! Is it okay to come inside?"

"We have no cooties," Natalia informed her, with eyes sparkling humorously over her mask.

"Promise!" Jazmine added.

The girls spent the day hanging out, playing with makeup and hairstyles and picking out a dress from the multitude the girls had brought with them. Unbeknownst to Zoey, they'd been instructed to keep her occupied and away from the back of the house.

"So where are we starting?" Quinn asked, Jericho as she walked into the backyard.

"We've already started," Dakota informed the Irishwoman.

"Where've you been?" Raine asked, as she strung lights from the fence.

"I scored the champagne and beer," Quinn retorted, making a face at the other two women. Raine and Dakota both stuck their tongues out at Quinn.

"Alright kids, no fights please," Jericho told them.

The other three laughed.

"No promises," Quinn informed Jericho.

By the time Zoey emerged that evening, their backyard had been transformed into a fairy garden of twinkling white and blue lights. She was completely dazzled.

"You look amazing," Jericho told her as she took her hand, bending at the waist to kiss the back of it gallantly. Zoey wore an A-line gown of white lace bodice with a slate blue tule skirt.

"You look hot!" Zoey exclaimed, her eyes sweeping over her handsome fiancée. Jericho was dressed in a black well-cut suit with a white starched shirt and black dress cowboy boots. There was a round of chuckles from their guests.

"So obviously everyone couldn't make it," Jericho told Zoey, waving her arm toward the three couples that had been at that house already. They had been joined by Wynter and Remi—who was still using a cane to walk at that point. "Our yard isn't big enough for too many people and others haven't been in quarantine long enough, so they're joining us via the internet, thanks to Harley."

Jericho gestured to the camera that had been placed on the gazebo in the back yard. Zoey waved.

"What about your parents?" Zoey asked, suddenly worried that the Tehrani's wouldn't get to see their only daughter get married.

"They're here too, it's early where they are, but they're watching." Jericho said, happy that Zoey had been concerned. "So are your parents."

"This is so great!" Zoey enthused, her smile wide, as she waved at the camera. "Thank you guys for this!"

"We also have an officiant," Jericho said, gesturing to the laptop on the podium under the gazebo. BJ Sparks smiled from the laptop screen.

"Oh my gawd, hi!" Zoey waved at BJ, who laughed, waving back. "You thought of everything," Zoey told Jericho.

"Yep." Jericho nodded, even as Wynter handed Zoey a spray of white calla lilies and rainbow roses.

"Wow…" Zoey's eyes glazed with tears as she looked up at Jericho. "Thank you."

Jericho leaned in, kissing Zoey's lips softly. "Wanna get married now?"

"Sure, why not?" Zoey laughed softly.

The ceremony was short and sweet, the party went into the wee hours. At one point, Jericho and Zoey sat together, watching Dakota trying to outdrink Quinn.

"That's never going to happen," Jericho commented.

"Nope," Zoey agreed.

"Oh, by the way," Jericho said, leaning in to nuzzle her wife's neck, "we'll be having a real party later on, this is just the legal part."

"That's not necessary," Zoey told her, "the legal part was what I wanted."

"Well, we deserve the party too," Jericho told her with a smile.

"Yes, dear," Zoey answered.

"Oh and a honeymoon too. Post pandemic, of course."

"Of course." Zoey rolled her eyes.

"I saw that."

"Uh-huh."

August 6, 2020

Finley had come down with cold symptoms three days after she tested positive for COVID. She ran a fever for three days. Kai checked on her constantly.

"How are you this morning?" Kai asked as she knocked on the spare bedroom door. It was day four and she hated that she couldn't see her fiancée when she was sick.

Finley turned over in bed and did a quick self-assessment. "Better, actually."

On her side of the door, Kai felt relief surge through her. "That's great! Do you want breakfast?"

"Um, just tea for now, okay?" Finley wasn't wanting to push it.

"Babe..." Kai entreated. "You need to eat to keep your strength up to fight this thing."

Finely grinned to herself, it's what she'd always tell her patients when they were recovering from surgery or illness. "My words coming back to haunt me, huh?"

"You got it!" Kai laughed. "How about something nice and simple, scrambled eggs with some cheese?"

"That sounds good, honey, thank you."

Finley reflected on her relationship with Kai. While she'd originally been unwilling to get involved with a butch woman because she was afraid they would be too controlling, Kai had taught her that someone could be protective without being overly dominating. It was a bit of a learning curve for Finley and she'd almost lost Kai with her stubbornness; thankfully Jackie had intervened and had seen to it that they'd gotten a chance to talk. It had been that talk that had gotten them together once and for all. Now Finley couldn't imagine her life without this wonderful woman in her life. Kai Temple was definitely the perfect partner for her: strong, but willing to bend, protective, but accepting of Finley's job and independent streak. Their relationship was both loving and supportive in all the right ways. Finley thanked the Fates that had drawn them together.

Twenty minutes later, they ate breakfast, each on their own side of the door.

"So what's your day look like?" Finley asked conversationally.

Kai hesitated, "I uh... I'll be here."

"You don't have to babysit me honey."

"You are mine to take care of," Kai said simply.

On her side Finley smiled softly, feeling her heart swell at Kai's words.

"Okay," she answered simply, because emotion was clogging her throat. She had to admit it felt good to have Kai there to look out for her.

August 7, 2020

"Can you repeat that?" Midnight asked, looking at her computer screen. They'd suspended most in person meetings; they were using Teams online to keep up with Midnight's schedule.

Marilyn grimaced. "Our numbers may not be going down."

Midnight stared back at the woman for a long moment, blinking slowly. "What happened?" she asked simply.

Marilyn shook her head, "We didn't get an agreement renewal done on time with Quest Labs, so we didn't get the data from Quest for July thirty-first through August fourth"What does that mean?" Midnight asked.

"We needed to do a contract renewal with the company, and we failed to do that on time," Marilyn explained.

Midnight took a deep calming breath, trying to overcome the desire to scream. They thought they were finally getting ahead, but now, maybe not. She knew it wouldn't do any good to rage, but she really wanted to at that moment.

"So you'll get me the accurate numbers, when?" she prompted instead.

"As soon as possible ma'am," Marilyn told her.

"Good."

"Bondye…" Remi hissed through gritted teeth as she did her best to push the weight bar away from her chest.

"Blow your breath out as you push, remember?" Kai warned gently. They were at the gym. It had taken hours for Finley to talk her into going. Remi had wanted to start working on getting her strength back. It had been nearly four months since she'd returned from England, and it was slow going and she hated it.

"I'm trying!" Remi grouched.

"It's going to take time," Kai told her, "you'll get there."

Remi through her a doubtful look but continued to lift the weight for the ten reps Kai had ordered her to do. "How is Fin?" Everyone was worried about Finley; she was the caretaker for everyone else and now she was sick.

Kai nodded, looking circumspect. "So far she's really doing good, just cold symptoms, but she feels better every day."

"Sa bon, that's good," Remi nodded.

The group had responded in force to hearing that Finley had COVID: flowers, gifts, phone calls and emails had poured in. The outpouring of love and support had really warmed both of their hearts.

Remi had also received a great deal of attention due to her hospitalization and continuing health issues due to COVID. It embarrassed the humble fighter, but she appreciated that people cared about her. Her road to recovery had definitely been arduous—she'd finally gotten enough strength up to start training again, but even then she wasn't happy with how weak her muscles still were. She hoped working with Kai would help her focus in the right areas to assist her in getting back her fighting strength.

August 9, 2020

"Marilyn, you don't have to do this," Midnight told the Director, as she held the woman's letter of resignation in her hands.

"I let you down," Marilyn stated simply.

Midnight sighed audibly, shaking her head, "I don't feel like you did."

"It's my responsibility."

Midnight curled up her lips in disdain, she knew that it was someone under the Director that had screwed up, and she sincerely hoped that person got fired, but didn't feel like Marilyn should have to take the blame.

"Are you sure about this?" Midnight asked.

"They're already starting to blame you for 'false hope' and saying that you lied to make it look like you were doing a good job." Marilyn looked incredibly unhappy at that point. "I never wanted to let you down like this."

"It's a freaking pandemic!" Midnight raged. "No one has a rule book for this. Shit happens!"

Marilyn laughed softly, appreciating that Midnight Chevalier wasn't like most politicians that would have demanded her head on a plate. The Governor was definitely a class act.

August 21, 2020

"How many can we count on then?" Gage asked, knowing her impatience was showing, but with too tired to mask it.

"I'm hearing that we'll only be able to staff ninety of the crews at this point." Hunter told the director of OES, cringing, because she knew it wasn't going to be enough.

The inmate fire crew that were usually one hundred and ninety-two crews strong, were down due to the pandemic raging through the inmate populations. With around three hundred and fifty fires burning throughout the State, the much-needed help of inmates cutting fire lines to help slow down the infernos was going to be sorely missed.

Hunter heard Gage blow her breath out, wishing she'd had better news to give the other woman.

"That's less than half," Gage commented dismally.

"I know ma'am, I'm sorry."

"Not your fault Briggs, this pandemic is killing all of us—in more ways than one."

"You're not kidding!" Hunter readily agreed.

Chapter 6

850,402 Cases/ 17,041 Deaths in California
36,749,405 Cases Worldwide/1,140,156 Deaths

October 6, 2020

"How many totally acres burned?" Gage asked dumbfounded.

"Almost four hundred thousand," Kori replied, still in shock herself.

"This is just astounding."

"And not in a good way." Kori sighed.

"Nope," Gage replied, mirroring Kori's sigh, "I'll let Midnight know. This year just gets worse and worse."

"One big dumpster fire," Hunter put in. They were on a conference call with the Office of Emergency Services.

"We're already breaking records for acreage burned," Kori stated.

"We need to get ahead of resources for this," Gunn said from her end of the line in San Francisco. "Shenin, are tapped out on military aide do you think?"

"I've got a call in to a few people. We might be able to get some help," Shenin, who was on the call from she and Tyler's home.

"Let me know what you hear," Gage told Shenin. "If I need to get Midnight to make some calls, I can definitely ask."

"Got it." Shenin nodded.

"How's Aiden doing?" Gage asked, not having seen Shenin in months during the pandemic.

"Oh he's good, running around getting into everything!" Shenin laughed. "He got ahold of a bottle of hand sanitizer the other day, had it all over the couch. I thought Tyler was going to have heart failure."

"Oh they're so much fun at that age! Said no one ever," Gunn grumbled.

"Oh stop, don't you remember how much fun Mark was at that point?" Gage asked, glancing at Kit. Kit had never really said that the history she shared with Gunn bothered her, but it was always something Gage was careful about. It wasn't easy having had a history with one woman who was still your best friend, and your current wife knew her.

"Sure, right up until he figured out how to open the front door," Gunn answered.

"Oh, Jesus, bite your tongue!" Shenin exclaimed. "Ty will have the door padlocked if she hears about that."

"You mean she doesn't already?" Gage asked.

"I think she's too busy trying to child proof everything else," Shenin told them.

"Hey, how's the co-habiting going between Syd and Mia?" Kit asked from her side of Gage's desk at their house.

"Oh they're like little love birds," Gunn said, grinning, "Mia's decorating, and Syd's trying to talk her into her own game room."

"I'm sure Harley is helping with that argument," Shenin said.

"Oh yeah, she keeps sending Syd new articles about the latest and greatest systems with surround sound!" Gunn laughed, "I think Mia's considering shutting down their wi-fi at this point."

Everyone laughed, it was a relief to talk about something other than the utter devastation happening around them, both medically and environmentally. The California wildfires were raging out of control. The fire season had been horrendous already, and it wasn't showing any signs of letting up. They were all trying to cope in their own way.

October 10, 2020

"I'm pleased to announce that we're loosening restrictions on private gatherings." Midnight smiled for the first time in a while. She was happy to be able to hold this press conference, they were finally seeing light at the end of the tunnel. "We're below three percent on infection rates, and everything tells us this is on a downward trend. Thank you to everyone who has done their part to slow this virus!" Midnight wanted to comment about others who had been a pain in the ass during the last so many months but refrained. Everyone had informed her that she shouldn't do that.

"I saw that hesitation," Rick grinned as Midnight joined him at the edge of the stage.

"Shut it," Midnight muttered as they passed member of the press.

Rick simply laughed. He knew his wife well enough to know what she'd wanted to say.

"It's tough being so politically correct, ain't it?" he commented.

"Ya know..." Midnight's voice trailed off as she narrowed her eyes at him.

"Yes, love, I know." Midnight was sure she could hear the sardonic grin she was sure was on his lips behind the mask that he wore.

"You almost did it, didn't you?" Kana asked as she and Tiny fell into step behind the Debenshires.

Midnight threw up her hands. "The important thing is that I didn't, Jesus!"

"Didn't what?" Joe asked as he walked up.

"She almost went on a tirade," Rick put in.

"I did not!" Midnight snapped.

"Did too," Tiny commented.

Midnight stopped walking, almost causing Tiny and Kana to collide with her. "You people need to give me credit for not speaking my mind, it ain't always easy, ya know!"

She looked around at the people that currently surrounded her, she could feel the grins and pursed lips. These were her people, the people that she knew she could trust with her life. They'd been through hell and back with her, and she loved them all dearly. Finally, she just shook her head, her copper blonde curls flowing around her shoulders.

"If I have to see the end of the world, I guess I'm happy it's with you guys," she smiled, her eyes crinkling at the corners, "but I swear you're lucky they don't let me come to these press conferences armed anymore." She winked at her friends then continued on her way. People standing nearby were both surprised and amused by the scene. Governor Midnight Chevalier was definitely one of a kind!

***

"If things are loosening up, maybe we could go down in the new year," Raine commented.

She and Natalia were sitting on the couch in their apartment. They'd just watched the press conference Midnight had given saying restrictions were being loosened up. It had been a long year for them, like it had for everyone else. They'd planned to go down to Mexico in March so Raine could meet Natalia's parents and they could announce their engagement. They'd even discussed getting married in Mexico.

"If it's possible," Natalia said, "but I don't want to rush it."

"Why?" Raine asked, looking a bit hurt.

"Ah mi bebe, it is not you!" Natalia assured, touching Raine's face with her fingertips. "I want to make sure it is completely safe. My abuela is so fragile, I would be afraid to bring the virus to her."

Raine drew a breath in through her nose even as she nodded her understanding. Things had been good with them for the last three years, but there was always that sliver of doubt in Raine's mind. Natalia knew this and felt bad that she'd never be able to fully erase her moment of foolish weakness when she'd cheated on Raine. It was something she could never take back, and she knew that. She just did her best to put it behind them.

"Well, I guess we'll revisit the idea once the new year comes and if the border reopens."

191

Natalia put her head against Raine's chest, hoping that things would reopen fully soon.

October 15, 2020

"They're here," McKenna told Savanna.

Savanna looked up from her computer, smiling as she did. "Fantastic! Set them up in the sun room, I'll be out in just a minute. Thanks Kenna."

Walking back out to the foyer of the house, McKenna gestured to River and Fadiyah to follow her out to the sunroom.

"You guys can set up out here. I have a couple of tables that we can bring out, and some chairs. Do you think you'll need anything else?"

"That should be good, right Fadi?" River queried.

Fadiyah nodded. "It would probably be a good idea for them to have some juice or something too."

"Good idea," River agreed.

"Got it! Thank you two so much for doing this!" McKenna enthused. "You have no idea how much we need this right now."

River nodded, smiling over at Fadiyah.

"We're happy to help!" River told McKenna.

It had started with a conversation between Lyric and Jet. They'd been talking about motorcycles, which had turned into talk about how everyone in their households were doing. Then Lyric had mentioned how stressed Savanna was about not being able to get the kids in the home in to see anyone for minor issues and things like vaccinations and flu shots. Jet had taken it from there. Fadiyah and River had taken time out of their schedules to gather supplies to help out and today was their first "clinic". They even had Finley on speed dial in case there was anything they couldn't solve.

Savanna walked into the sun room a few minutes later. "You ladies are life savers!" she proclaimed.

"I am so glad we could help," Fadiyah told her, reaching out to hug Savanna, "how are things doing here?"

"Crazy!" Savanna laughed, shaking her head. "This pandemic is really affecting so many of these kids, we're completely overloaded and we have no way to keep them really entertained. They can't go anywhere safely and we have to quarantine anyone new, which is tough. The homeschooling is a nightmare!"

River shook her head. "I can't even imagine! I'd be going nuts right now if I was a parent."

"I'm really glad Ana isn't old enough to attend school yet," Savanna agreed.

"Another year or so, right?" River asked.

"Yep. Hopefully all this COVID craziness is done by then."

"Maybe when the vaccines become available?" Fadiyah put in hopefully.

"Sounds like they're getting closer," River said.

"There will still be idiots who won't get it," Savanna sighed, "just like the ones that refuse to wear a mask."

River and Fadiyah rolled their eyes, they'd both seen it enough at the hospitals where they worked.

"Speaking of which, let's get this vaccination show on the road!" River said.

After four hours, all twenty-five of the kids in the home had been given flu shots, vaccines or had been seen for various issues. Savanna and McKenna had set lunch for the two nurses, so grateful for their help. The four sat in the small eat in kitchen, talking.

"How's Cody doing?" River asked, knowing from Sinclair that a lot of undercover operations had been suspended during the pandemic.

"Going a bit stir crazy at this point." McKenna rolled her eyes. "She and Dakota are doing some remodeling on our house. I'm ready to kill them both."

"Sinclair is prowling the house constantly thinking up things to do too," River said.

"How is her grandfather doing?" Savanna asked.

"Alright, he's having some memory issues again, but we're working on it."

"Good." Savanna nodded. "Fadi how is Jet coping?"

"She is learning a new language again."

"What now?" McKenna asked, grinning.

"Well, she has perfected Farsi and Arabic, and now she's learning Portuguese."

"To communicate with Jovina, right?" River asked.

"Well, it was Jovina's use of the language that made Jet want to learn it, apparently."

Both Savanna and McKenna shook their heads, Jet was ADHD so needed to be busy all of the time. They didn't envy Fadiyah dealing with that on a daily basis.

"Have you and Lyric gone camping again?" Fadiyah asked.

"A couple of times, never anything as crazy as that first trip though!" Savanna sighed, shaking her head. "We've kept it fairly local, but Lyric is wanting to do another long trip to somewhere like Tahoe or farther north."

"That might be fun," River said.

"You weren't on that last trip!" Savanna huffed.

All four women laughed.

"So are you and Cody working on having that baby yet?" River queried.

"Not at this point!" McKenna shook her head. "I'm too chicken to get pregnant till this is all over with."

"I know! It is so scary!" Fadiyah agreed. "I know that Devin is terrified."

"I would be too!" River said.

They all nodded their heads, the idea of having to give birth without any family or friends around them sounded like their worst nightmare.

"When is she due?" McKenna asked.

"The end of April," Fadiyah told her.

"Let's hope some of this craziness has calmed down by then," Savanna said.

They all agreed whole heartedly with that.

November 7, 2020

Relief flooded Midnight's body as Joe Biden was pronounced the winner of the 2020 elections. It had been four stressful days since the election, and she had silently prayed that Biden would win.

Trump had actually continued to downplay the effects of the pandemic, even making fun of Biden for wearing a mask all the time. It had Midnight cringing constantly, she knew they needed strong leadership if they were ever going to emerge from the nightmare of COVID and she didn't feel that Donald Trump was that leader.

November 12, 2020

Unfortunately, by November cases in the United States were going up again. The United States hit an all-time high for diagnosed cases in a seven-day period of 150,000. On average, 1,000 people a week were dying of the virus. California hit one million cases. It didn't bode well for the people of the United States.

"Maybe they'll get the vaccine out soon," Ashley said to Sebastian over dinner that night.

Sebastian blew his breath out. As a normally staunch supporter of the Republican party, he felt very defeated by the current administration's antics. He was further horrified by the actions of the President himself.

"I'm just afraid people are going to travel for the holidays and it'll just get worse and worse," he said, having heard that it was the latest concern on the horizon that night on the news.

"Well, none of us are going anywhere," Ashley said, referring to the entire group. Many discussions had happened about having a gathering for Thanksgiving again, but they'd all decided it wasn't safe just yet.

"We'll just do something small," Sebastian said.

Ashley agreed, the last thing she wanted was for Sebastian or their son Benjamin to get sick. "Maybe we could have Kash and Sierra over?"

Sebastian thought about it. "I can talk to Kash, maybe if they can quarantine for the next two weeks, we can try."

Ashley smiled, nodding; she knew it would do her husband good to see his best friend. He'd been working from home, trying to keep track of his people and their cases, but things had been slow. He was getting antsy, having Kashena around for an evening would boost his spirits.

Sebastian called Kashena that evening.

"Yo Marine, how's it going?" he asked without preamble.

"This sucks," Kashena replied.

"Roger that. So, Ash was wondering if you and Sierra could come for Thanksgiving dinner? Any chance you and the wife could make that?"

Kashena narrowed her eyes at her end, mentally going over her schedule, and trying to remember if Sierra had any appearance to make in the next couple of weeks. "I think we might be able to. If I can get Colby to quarantine, can he come too?"

"Of course! It's been forever since I've seen him."

"Great, this will be nice!" Kashena said, things had been so horrible with the pandemic and not being able to see people and working from home all the time.

"Bring beer!" Sebastian grunted.

"Lots!" Kashena agreed.

November 26, 2020

Sebastian opened the door to his and Ashley's home, smiling at the small group that stood there. Kashena had asked if they could add Colby's new girlfriend—a different one from the previous year—since they'd been quarantining, and Colby was excited to introduce her around. Sebastian had happily agreed, after making sure that the girl had also been isolating for the two weeks as well. He was never willing to take a chance with his wife and child's health on the line.

"There they are!" Sebastian boomed, smiling broadly. "Where's the beer?" he asked winking.

"Right here, Ranger, let us in!" Kashena laughed, holding up the case of beer.

Sebastian took the case from her and stood aside to let them in, even as he reached out to shake Kashena's hand with a pirate's smile. Inside they stood in the foyer, Sierra reached up to hug Sebastian even as Ashley and their son Benjamin came into the room. There were hugs all around.

"Sebastian and Ashley," Colby began, his hand on the back of the small blonde girl next to him, "this is Sabrina. Sabrina, this is Special Agent in Charge, Sebastian Bach, and his wife Ashley, and that's Benjie." He pointed to the adorable blonde toddler.

The young woman nodded. "It's nice to meet you," she said, her voice soft.

"Good to meet you, Sabrina." Ashley smiled, glancing over at Sebastian. She could see he was sizing the girl up, trying to determine if she was good enough for Colby.

"Bas, stop it," she warned.

Sebastian just grinned unrepentantly, even as Kashena rolled her eyes.

"Come on in," Ashley gestured toward the living room.

"Nice…" Kashena whistled, her eyes on the new entertainment center in the spacious living room.

Sebastian smiled proudly, "I've had a lot of time on my hands."

"Right?" Kashena queried, "So much frigging time!"

The conversation devolved into all the projects they were working on, much to the exclusion of everyone else in the room.

"Wine?" Ashley offered Sierra.

"Yes please!" Sierra exclaimed.

"You two can head into the den, there's a TV in there," Ashley told Colby and Sabrina. "Come on Bennie!" she told the toddler.

In the kitchen Ashley poured Sierra some wine, and they sat talking in the breakfast nook.

"So how are things?" Ashley asked.

"They're alright," Sierra smiled, "I mean, as well as can be expected with this craziness going on."

"Yeah, this is definitely one for the record books," Ashley agreed. "Didn't Colby graduate in June?"

"Yes he did, but it was certainly not what I was expecting for my son's graduation."

"Oh yeah, how did that work?"

"They did this kind of a drive-by kind of ceremony," Sierra explained, "we were in the car and the kids got to walk across this little stage and stand there with their certificates so we could get pictures. It was weird."

"Yikes!" Ashley looked shocked. "I'll bet."

Sierra shrugged. "He didn't seem to mind, he was just happy to be done with high school."

"Oh, I'm sure!" Ashley laughed. "What's he planning to do now? Is he starting college?"

Sierra grimaced. "Oh, no that was another whole argument."

"What happened?"

"He wants to 'experience life' first," Sierra said using air quotes, "Kashena was not thrilled."

Ashley's eyes widened as she bit her lower lip.

"I can only imagine." She was well aware of her husband as well as his best friend's work ethic. "So what's going to happen?"

"Well, apparently Colby's idea of 'experiencing life' was laying around playing video games, so Kashena gave him a deadline of June next year. Either he gets his proverbial shit together or she's signing him up for the Marines."

Ashley's mouth dropped open as she blinked repeatedly. "Wow!"

Sierra shrugged. "He's been around Kashena long enough to know that she wouldn't go for him being a bum. I just hope this pandemic is over before I have to take him to basic training."

Ashley laughed, "You don't think he'll change his mind and sign up for college before then?"

"I think he better get smart fast." Sierra rolled her eyes.

"Now is this the same girlfriend from last year?" Ashley asked.

Sierra chuckled, "Oh no, this an all new one."

"I just remember Kashena being really unhappy with Colby about him not coming to the group dinner."

Sierra pressed her lips together. "Well, to be fair, she knew that I wasn't happy about him choosing her family over ours," she intimated, "but I was trying to downplay it."

"I don't think Kashena Wind-Walker knows how to downplay things," Ashley stated.

Sierra clinked her wine glass with Ashley's. "You got that right. The girl really was a bit of a snob though, so I'm glad he's not with her anymore."

"Oh we don't do snobs, that's for sure!" Ashley laughed.

"How are you and Sebastian doing?" Sierra asked.

"We're good," Ashley smiled, "except for him going stir crazy and doing a hundred and one home improvement projects. It makes it a bit hard to work, you know?"

"You're doing a blog now, aren't you?" Sierra queried, having heard that information from Kashena.

"Yes, the newspaper wants me to document the ways that California is responding to the pandemic. I got lucky with you all being so close to the Governor, so I'm getting first-hand information. It's great!"

Sierra nodded happily. "I know Midnight is all about transparency. She wants people to know what's happening."

"That's so true, it's fantastic to get it straight from her and her office. I feel like it's so important right now."

"That it is!" Sierra agreed.

Later at dinner, Sebastian and Kashena started talking about their time together in the military. It was definitely entertaining.

"It wasn't my fault!" Sebastian insisted.

"You don't know how a flashbang works...or?" Kashena prompted with a wide grin.

"Just shut it, Marine, okay?" Sebastian made a face at his long-time friend, as everyone else at the table laughed.

"Got it, Ranger, got it." Kashena laughed, holding up her beer in a salute.

"So you were both in the military?" Sabrina asked, having finally found her voice.

"Yep," Sebastian nodded.

"But you weren't both Marines?"

"Nope," Sebastian took a drink, "I was too smart to be a Marine." He winked at Kashena, who only rolled her eyes. "I was an Army Ranger."

"Is that better?" Sabrina asked.

"Hell no!" Kashena exclaimed, even as the rest of the table started to chuckle. That's when Kashena saw the barely contained impudent grin on the younger woman's face. "Aww, got me there, didn't you?" Kashena decided then that she liked this new girl.

December 1, 2020

"I don't like this..." Kana grumbled, as Midnight's group arrived at the warehouse.

They were there to see the efforts being put in by volunteers to pack food and essentials for people who needed help during the pandemic. It was obvious, however, that some of Midnight's critics had gotten word she'd be there as there was a full-blown protest occurring in front of the location.

"Oh that one's charming," Midnight pointed out, referring to a bright orange sign that read: "Sacrifice the weak and reopen CA" in block lettering. "These people are unreal!"

"Did they miss that the Stay at Home order has been lifted for months?" Tiny asked from the back seat.

"They aren't exactly creative," Midnight commented, "they were probably so proud of that sign that they just keep using it." Her tone indicated her disgust with the sign as well as the sign holder.

"Let's keep things close, here, okay?" Kana said as she parked the vehicle in the area that had been cordoned off for their group.

Kana got out of the vehicle first, going around the front of the large SUV to Midnight's side of the car. Tiny came around the back of the vehicle, standing at the rear passenger door. Midnight climbed out of the vehicle from the front passenger side.

As they proceeded forward, the man running one of the volunteer groups came forward to speak with them. He wore a red face mask. As he extended his hand to Midnight, another man came walking up behind the first.

"Governor, it's nice to meet you," the man began, only to have the other man rush forward.

This man was not wearing a mask, and attempted to get right into Midnight's face, yelling, "No mask mandates!"

He was quickly blocked by Kana, with Tiny not far behind. When the man attempted to go around Kana, she grabbed him up by two handfuls of his jacket and, lifting him off his feet, backed him away from Midnight. Tiny quickly moved forward to protect

Midnight, as her back up detail moved in to protect her from behind.

"You have no right to put your hands on me!" the man screamed into Kana's face, getting spit on her mask and face as he did.

Kana didn't respond, simply pushing him up against the nearest wall and holding him there as the Sacramento Police Department moved in to respond. Wiping her face as she walked away, she heard the officers telling him he was under arrest for attempted assault on the Governor.

"You okay?" Tiny asked Kana as she reclaimed her position.

"Yeah fasi mea leaga," she commented as she gestured back toward the man the police were arresting, calling him a piece of shit in Samoan.

"Tonu," Tiny agreed, saying 'exactly' in their native tongue.

The two, nicknamed the Samoan Express, had vowed to protect Midnight with their lives, and they'd meant it. They didn't take kindly to anyone who tried to hurt the tiny powerhouse of a Governor. Tiny and Kana had been with Midnight from nearly the beginning of her career, she'd saved their lives a few times, and they took that very seriously.

A short while later, while Midnight was safely touring the facility, a police sergeant flagged Kana down, pulling her aside.

"Ma'am," the sergeant began, his blue eyes expressing remorse for what he needed to tell her, "the man you dealt with informed us that he's positive for COVID, apparently he was attempting to infect the Governor."

"Son of a…" Kana muttered, shaking her head. "I hope you're charging him with attempted murder too then."

"Yes, ma'am," the sergeant affirmed, "but you should definitely get tested. I know you're wearing a mask, but he was spitting as he yelled, and I saw he got you in the face…" his voice trailed off as he grimaced. "You could be infected."

Kana scowled.

"So two attempts of murder," she growled, even as she started figuring out how to proceed. She definitely didn't want to be around Midnight if she might be infected. Pulling out her phone, she texted Tiny to let him know what was going on.

She received a one-word reply: "Fuck!"

That same day, everyone in the group received the special delivery of an invitation. The invitation itself was very fancy, in gold, burgundy and deep green. The handwritten card was from Brenden and Allexxiss Sparks and read: "Please join us at our home to celebrate Christmas day and evening!" The invitation also detailed instructions on self-isolating prior to the holiday.

December 6, 2020

Less than a week after the incident, Kana tested positive for COVID. Her symptoms came in the form of extreme fatigue and muscle aches. She had to isolate herself from Palani and their five-year-old daughter, Anone. Midnight was doubly irate about protestors at that point, and it took everything she had not to scream bloody murder at them whenever they protested at any of her events. Tiny carefully controlled the Governor, utilizing the assistance of her husband and their longtime friends Joe Sinclair and John Machiavelli.

Fortunately, Kana's symptoms only lasted a week and abated quickly, much to Palani's relief.

December 14, 2020

Finley barely felt the needle go into her upper arm, but she felt relief flood her veins as did the vaccine. She, with many of her fellow medical workers were receiving their very first vaccine against COVID19, they all hoped against hope that this was the beginning of the end to the pandemic.

December 25, 2020

"Come on in!" BJ said, not for the first time that morning. "How's it going?"

"It's going alright," Memphis said, smiling behind her mask even as she looked around her.

The foyer in the Sparks home was decorated to the hilt for Christmas, not the least of which was a twenty-foot Christmas tree that sparkled and winked with beautiful blue and white decorations.

"Wow, that's some tree…" Memphis whistled, as Kieran nodded her agreement.

"Allexxiss had a team of decorators out here for days!" BJ admitted, laughing. "Come on into the living room, your protectors are already here." He winked at Memphis to show there were no hard feelings. Quinn had lit into him about harassing Memphis for another album, Remington had backed her up.

Memphis pressed her lips together in consternation, even as she and Kieran walked into the living room. They removed their masks as they did, seeing that everyone else there weren't wearing any. Remi, Wynter, Quinn and Xandy were standing near the fireplace. Walking over to the group, Memphis leaned into Quinn, who put her arm around the smaller woman.

"We talked to him," Quinn told Memphis.

"I heard," Memphis answered.

"What did he say?" Remington asked, her eyes clouding with worry.

"He was fine," Kieran put in, "he just commented that her protectors were already here."

"Was he okay with me not doing another album?" Memphis practically squeaked.

"He said he just wanted you to do what you loved, and if that wasn't singing, then he'd leave you alone about it," Wynter told Memphis. "You really just needed to tell him, hon."

Memphis drew in a deep breath, blowing it out slowly as she nodded. "Stop being a chicken," she said, her tone self-effacing.

"Hey!" Xandy exclaimed. "He scares the bejeepers out of me too!"

"I do what?" BJ asked, raising a dark auburn eyebrow, his tone sharp.

"Quit it," Allexxiss told him as she walked up, elbowing him in the ribs gently, which had him chuckling. "He just loves you

Memphis," she intimated, "and he really just wants the best for you. He just thinks that everyone wants to be famous."

"I don't," Memphis shook her head to back up her statement.

"Duly noted," BJ said, rolling his eyes dramatically.

"Go answer the door," Allexxiss said as the doorbell chimed again.

"We do have people for this," BJ told her.

"Go… answer… the… door…" Allexxiss repeated, her words measured this time.

BJ sighed, walking away. The group snickered; it was funny to see such a powerful man cowed by his equally powerful wife. They knew that BJ Sparks loved his wife more than anything in the world, so he would take it from her, if no one else.

The Falco's arrived next, adding to the level of mayhem in the living room as drinks were served. Dakota and Cody were, as always, bickering over the result of the race to the house in their respective Ferraris.

"Admit it, I beat you," Cody told her adopted sister.

"In a pig's eye!" Dakota replied.

"Girls…" Savanna sighed. "Can we just call it a tie?"

"No!" Both women answered, causing a laugh through the group.

"Don't make me split you two up," Lyric warned with a grin.

"Blah, blah, blah," Cody sing-songed, rolling her eyes.

"Behave yourself!" McKenna told her wife.

"Yes dear," Cody answered.

"Yes dear," Dakota mimicked, only to get poked in the ribs by Jazmine.

BJ was still shaking his head when he answered the door again minutes later.

"Aw, it's my favorite actresses." He smiled as he welcomed Riley and Talon, followed closely by Legend and Parker. "And my favorite director and cop." BJ finished, winking as if he'd always meant to say that too.

"Yeah, yeah," Legend laughed, "you say that now."

"Gonna give me back my music producer anytime soon?" BJ queried.

"Nope," Legend informed him, with a twinkle in her eyes.

"Then I take it back," BJ commented.

"Jesus H Christ, look at this place!" Sebastian stood staring up at the Sparks home, his mouth hanging open.

"Yeah, wow," Ashley agreed, they'd been surprised to be invited, and had of course been thrilled to actually have dinner with a world-renowned rock star, as well as his movie star wife.

"Rubbing elbows with the rich and famous now…" Kashena breathed as she and Sierra walked up with Colby and Sabrina in tow.

"God help us!" Sebastian widened his eyes.

"This is so exciting!" Sabrina enthused.

"Tell me about it!" Colby agreed.

"Is someone going to ring the bell, or are they supposed to divine that we're out here?" Sierra batted her eyelashes at her wife, even as she smiled broadly.

"I got it." Sebastian leaned in pressing the bell. "They're just people, right?" Sebastian was saying, just as the door was opened by Allexxiss. "Holy Hell…" he breathed.

"Hi!" Allexxiss enthused. "Come on in, I'm Allex." she continued, even as she extended her hand to the new arrivals.

"Um, yeah…" Sebastian nodded, looking completely starstruck.

"I'm Ashley, this is my husband Sebastian and our son Benjamin." Ashley recovered quickly, taking Allex's hand and squeezing it gently. "Thank you so much for this lovely invitation!"

"Of course!" Allexxiss said. "You're so welcome. Oh my god, he's so adorable!" she exclaimed, smiling brightly at the little boy. "Merry Christmas!" she said to him.

"Merry kiss-mas," Benjamin replied shyly.

"So handsome!" Allex enthused, then winked at Sebastian. "I'm sure it's good genes."

"I… yes ma'am." Sebastian stammered, his eyes looking like he was in some kind of a trance.

"Priceless!" Kashena laughed at the look on her long-time partner's face. "I think he's starstruck," she informed Allexxiss.

"Oh, you're Kashena Windwalker, aren't you?" Allex asked, her look a bit awed too.

"Yes ma'am," Kashena nodded, not understanding Allex's look, "this is my wife Sierra, our son Colby and his girlfriend Sabrina."

"It's so great to meet you," Allex nodded to the others, but her look went right back to Kashena. "I understand that you have premonitions, is that right?"

"I… yes ma'am," it was Kashena's turn to stammer.

"That is so interesting!" Allex clapped her hands together, her eyes sparkling. "I'm getting ready for a role where I play an intuitive, I would really love to pick your brain later if you're willing."

Kashena blinked a couple of times, unable to formulate words in the face of such a request.

"We call it 'the sight,'" Sierra informed Allex gently, trying to give Kashena a minute to recover.

Allex nodded, her gaze falling on Kashena again.

"Have I offended you?" she asked, her tone worried but her look sincere.

Kashena snapped out of her reverie. "No, ma'am, no, I'm just a bit surprised is all."

"Why?" It was an honest question but Allex couldn't fathom what Kashena meant, maybe she really was offended.

"Well, you're… world famous, I wouldn't think you'd need someone like me…"

"Like you?" Allex queried, "I'd say you're pretty well known yourself. I mean, didn't you save Midnight Chevalier and her bodyguards a few years back with your sight?"

When Kashena couldn't think of a way of answering without sounding boastful, Sierra stepped in. "Yes, she did."

Allex nodded smiling brightly. "There you go. I'm sorry, come in, please!"

The group stepped inside, finding themselves as amazed by the foyer as others had. Two stories high, the amazing tree next to the sweeping stairs highlighted the grandeur of the mansion.

Allex, having realized she'd overwhelmed the other woman, put her hand on Kashena's arm, and smiled. "We'll talk."

Kashena simply nodded, following the movie star into the living room where everyone stood talking.

A couple of hours later, almost everyone had arrived at the mansion. Waiters wearing masks and white gloves brought out trays and trays of hors d'oeuvres.

"So how is Cedars?" River was asking Fadiyah. "We're getting over-run."

"It is bad there too," Fadiyah told her.

As nurses, they hadn't been able to quarantine for the two weeks, but they'd been meticulous about their PPE, and had been tested repeatedly to ensure that they carried no infection into BJ's home.

"Finley is full recovered from her brush with COVID hasn't she?" Sinclair asked Fadiyah.

"Oh yes, she is all better, thankfully!" Fadiyah said, casting her eyes heavenward as if thanking Allah himself.

"Yeah, that was scary," Jet put in, shaking her head, "I wish Kai had been able to go back and deck the guy, for infecting Fin."

Fadiyah cast her eyes downward. "The man died."

"Justice served then," Sinclair commented. Fadiyah's eyes widened, even as Jet nodded in agreement. "Sorry, Fadi, but people who have no concern for anyone other than themselves, deserve what they get."

"It's called natural selection," Catalina put in, looking far from apologetic.

"Catalina!" Jovina exclaimed aghast, even as she crossed herself.

"What babe?" Catalina queried, "These people think it's okay to endanger everyone else, because they're too selfish to wear a mask. As far as I'm concerned, if your god wants to take 'em out, then so be it."

Jovina shook her head. She knew that Cat was not a believer of religion or God, so she knew it shouldn't surprise her, but somehow it had.

"What did you do now, Cat?" Rayden asked as she and Gray joined their small group.

"Said that the guy that infected Fin deserved what he got." Cat shrugged.

Rayden looked at the others. "Did he die?" The rest of the group nodded; Rayden put up her hand in a dismissive gesture. "Karma."

"Yup." Cat nodded again.

"He practically attacked Fin, too, right?" Gray asked.

"Yeah, he did," Sinclair answered.

It was Gray's turn to shrug. "Then yeah, he got what he deserved."

"Better that he died from the Rona, and not at Kai's hands," Rayden commented, her look circumspect.

"Well, that's true," Jovina agreed with that statement.

"What are we agreeing to over here?" Jericho asked as she and Zoey walked up.

"That it was better that the guy that got Fin sick died from the virus, rather than being taken apart by Kai," Catalina answered, smiling in mock innocence.

"Oh yeah," Jericho agreed rolling her eyes, "that would have been messy."

"And we'd have been getting Kai out of the country," Zoey added.

The group laughed at that comment.

"We'd have needed Midnight for that," Jericho said.

"Speaking of Midnight, is she coming today?" Zoey asked.

"Why, so you can talk to her about that program of yours?" Jericho asked, her grin wide.

"Maybe..." Zoey pressed her lips together, doing her best to look innocent.

"Dunno," Jericho shook her head, "did anyone hear if Kana is okay?"

"Yeah, she's fine," Cat said, "I talked to her the other day, that's someone else I would have helped take out if she'd gotten worse." Cat's eyes narrowed at the thought of Kana getting sick. She and Kana had remained friends over the years, and the idea of her friend dying from this horrible virus because she'd been doing her job made Cat madder than hell.

"That was because of a protestor, right?" Sinclair asked.

"Yeah, the fucker," Cat muttered.

"Tell us how you really feel," Jericho said, winking at Cat.

"I know, you're so closed up, Cat." Zoey laughed.

"She really is," Jovina added, squeezing Cat's hand that was in hers. Cat simply grinned in response.

"Anyway!" Cat went on, giving them all dirty looks. "Midnight isn't coming today because she's finally taking a little time to spend with her family. That's what Kana told me."

Everyone nodded, it made sense. Midnight Chevalier had been mired in the State's COVID response for months and months, without a break.

"It's good she's finally taking a break," Jericho commented.

"Yeah," Cat nodded, "I think that scare with Kana really put things in perspective for her."

"From what I heard, the guy was trying to give the virus to Midnight," Rayden said.

"Yeah," Cat confirmed, "the cops said that he figured if he gave it to Midnight and she recovered, it would prove that the virus wasn't that deadly."

"Crazy!" River exclaimed.

"These people are crazy," Sinclair told her.

"No, they're just stupidly following a man that uses gaslighting like it's second nature," Zoey explained.

The group nodded. Everyone had heard the reports that psychologists were saying that Trump was a sociopath and that he suffered from a narcissistic personality disorder. One psychoanalyst had stated that Trump was incapable of attending to any issue beyond his own personal need for adulation. It explained a lot about the man's response to the virus. It was damned scary!

"Grab him!" Shenin called to Tyler, as Aiden made a beeline for the living room and the groups gathered there.

Tyler went after the toddler, as Shenin smiled at BJ. "Sorry, he's gone straight from standing up to running in minutes."

BJ chuckled. "That's what happens."

"Don't say that!" Devin, who'd walked in with Skyler right behind Shenin, Tyler and Aiden.

"She's freaking out about the baby, obviously," Skyler explained to BJ.

"Oh it just gets better and better." BJ winked at them.

Devin pursed her lips, narrowing her eyes at BJ, "Why do I think you're lying to me on this one?"

BJ simply smiled, his light blue green eyes sparkling with humor as he raised his eyebrows a couple of times.

In the living room Aiden made it all the way to Zoey, who picked him up happily. Tyler caught up a few moments later.

"Ah-ha!" Tyler said, giving her son a narrowed look. "Found your girlfriend I see."

Zoey hugged the toddler to her. "He knows where to come!"

Tyler laughed, nodding. "Yeah, he's pretty smart like that. Heads into the room with all the pretty women."

"Just like his mother," Shenin put in as she walked up.

"You or me?" Tyler asked with a smile.

"Hmm, now that is the true question," Shenin answered, making everyone chuckle.

"Anyone seen Harley yet?" Rayden asked.

"For that matter, where are Raine and Nat, or Fin and Kai?" Zoey queried.

"No idea," Jericho said, shaking her head.

"Did Gage and Kit make it?" Shenin asked, looking around the huge living room.

"Not that I've seen." Catalina shook her head.

"We've been so buried with the fires, we're lucky any of us made it," Shenin said.

"Yeah they're bad," Jovina said, having been watching the news reports about all the fires in California at that point. "We just can't catch a break."

"Harley, slow down, please," Shiloh said, as her girlfriend took another curve and top speed. "BJ won't show the other bois his cars till we're all there, okay?"

"You don't know that." Harley grinned, finding it amusing that Shiloh knew exactly what she was excited about.

"I know if you wreck this car again, you'll be mad as hell."

"True," Harley agreed. It had taken a lot of work to get her Z back on the road, she was just happy to be driving it again.

"Glad you could make it," BJ told Gage as she and Kit walked in.

"Not sure how long we'll be here," Gage told him, "shit just keeps going off!"

"Understandable. Welcome regardless. Any chance your San Francisco staff will make it down?"

"No, there's been too many outbreaks there recently, they send their regards though." Gage told him.

BJ nodded, understanding the concern. He and Allex hadn't even been sure this get together was possible, but they'd been surprised when nearly everyone had RSVP'd.

"This is loco…" Natalia breathed as she and Raine walked up to the door.

"Yeah, it's a bit surreal," Raine agreed, even as she rang the doorbell.

When BJ Sparks himself opened the door, both women froze, unable to formulate a word in the face of the fame they were suddenly in the presence of.

"Are you comin' in?" BJ asked with a smile.

"I, yes, um, thank you," Raine stammered.

Natalia eyed BJ as she walked into the foyer, then her eyes were drawn to the Christmas Tree. "Aye Dios Mio!" she exclaimed, making BJ laugh.

"She's a big one!" BJ agreed.

"Es Maravillos!" Natalia gasped.

"She says it's marvelous," Raine translated at BJ's confused look.

"Thanks for the assist." He winked.

"We are so late," Finley worried as she and Kai strode up to the house, hand in hand.

"It's okay, love," Kai assured her.

"There were just too many things to tie up."

"Hey, they let you work in the office and away from people. I'm not going to complain." Kai held up her free hand. "Let's just enjoy this day."

Finley nodded, leaning into Kai, as a way of apologizing for making them late.

218

Allexxiss opened the door with a flourish as they walked up. "Finally!" she exclaimed, shocking Finley. "Come in, come in!"

Finley looked over at Kai, expecting to see the confusion she was experiencing reflected on Kai's face, but it wasn't there. Kai was smiling at Allexxiss Ramsey Sparks like they were old friends.

"What the—" Finley started to say.

"Too much to do, not enough time for questions!" Allex interrupted, taking Finley's hand and tugging her into the house. "Come with me!"

Finley glanced back at Kai, but the woman was talking to BJ. Before she knew it, Finley was led up the staircase, and into a room that was absolutely huge. It was some sort of parlor with couches, and chairs set in semi-circles and a bar set up in the corner. Allex went directly to the bar and poured a glass of champagne, bringing it over to Finley; two women walked into the room.

"Uh, what's going on?" Finley asked, feeling like she was suddenly in an episode of the Twilight Zone.

"Well," Allex clasped her hands in front of her, as she glanced at the other women, "we're here to get you ready."

"For..." Finley prompted.

"Your wedding." Allex smiled warmly.

"My what?" Finley asked dumbly.

"Well, you see, Kai and I were talking, and—"

"When did you talk to Kai?" Finley queried sharply.

"When she was acting as my trainer," Allex answered, "anyway, I was asking when you two were going to get married, and she said that you were likely never going to. Because you're always

219

so busy there's no time to plan a wedding." Allex smiled winningly again. "So I decided to give you one."

Finley blinked a couple of time, trying to catch up. "Today," she finally said.

"Today."

"On Christmas."

"Yes." Allex smiled again, looking amused at Finley's confusion.

Finley was silent for a moment, trying to figure out exactly how she was in this predicament. She had a suspicious feeling that Kai had everything to do with it.

"Wearing this?" Finley asked, gesturing to the simple green dress she wore.

"No." Allex shook her head and gestured at the ladies who'd been hovering nearby. "Sally and Jennifer have brought you a selection of dresses from the best collections. All you have to do is try on and pick."

Finley's eyes widened. "Pick?"

"Yes," Allex said. Even as Finley heard the word, the door to the room opened and two trolleys of dresses were wheeled into the room.

"You've got to be kidding me," Finley breathed, even as Allex lead her over to the dresses.

"No ma'am," Allex told her, having the ladies start pulling dresses from the rack to show Finley.

Meanwhile, Kai and BJ stood downstairs in the foyer. Kai's gaze was on the door to the room the dresses had just gone through.

"Think she's gonna kill me?" Kai asked.

BJ chuckled. "From what you've told Allex, your beloved will be relieved she doesn't have to deal with planning."

It was true, Finley was really the kind of woman to happily go off to Vegas and 'get it over with'. They'd actually talked about eloping a few times, before the pandemic had it, but they'd just never taken the time.

Kai grimaced. "I just hope I wasn't wrong."

"Well, she hasn't come running out of the room cussing at you," BJ observed.

"True. Maybe the dresses slowed her down." Kai grinned.

"Speaking of which, you need to pick something out too. Come with me," BJ told her.

Two hours later, everyone had been informed that there was going to be a wedding that day. A team of workers had decorated the foyer further with burgundy and ivory tule and flowers galore. Seating had been placed facing the beautiful leaded glass windows of BJ's front doors. An aisle of burgundy velvet had been laid and the flowers continued along the chairs. Sprays of burgundy, mauve and peach-colored flowers of every type and texture adorned intricately woven gold flower stands. These flower stands were placed around the foyer, adding to the celebratory décor. After everyone got over the shock of that announcement, they'd been thrilled at the prospect of finally witnessing Kai and Finley get married. There were plenty of conversations about not having known so they could buy gifts, but BJ informed them all that there would be plenty of time for that later.

An hour later, Finley appeared at the top of the staircase, her hand in the crook of her mother's arm. She was dressed in an ivory Marchesa gown with a waterfall layered skirt and a corset bodice with dropped sleeves of embroidered lace. Her blonde hair was swept up in an elegant French twist with tendrils escaping around her face. Riley wore a silk gown of burgundy. The music began, played by the small trio of musicians BJ had hired for the occasion.

"Wow..." Kai breathed.

"Steady," Remington, who stood next to her as her best woman, told her.

Both women wore tuxedos cut perfectly with burgundy ties and vests.

The rest of the group looked on from chairs that had been placed around the staircase, and BJ stood waiting for Finley's arrival in front of the elegant doors to the front of the house.

Finley and Riley descended the stairs carefully, with Finley chanting, "Don't trip, don't trip, don't trip," under her breath the entire way down.

At the bottom of the stairs, Kai stepped over to take Finley's hand from Riley and she and Remi escorted Finley to BJ.

"And here we are," BJ commented, smiling at Kai and Finley as Remi stepped away, going to sit with Wynter in the front row. "So, we're here to these two married, finally!" There was a chuckle that went through the crowd. "It's my dear wife's understanding that Finley needed a little assistance in accomplishing this."

Finley dropped her head, shaking it, even as she grinned.

"S'okay," BJ intimated, "Allex loves to plan parties! So with that in mind, let's do this, so we can get to the food."

Fifteen minutes later, Kai and Finley were pronounced married.

"I'm getting good at this," BJ commented to his wife as they watched the group eat and drink and celebrate.

"Ya giving up music then?" Allexxiss asked him with a grin.

"Nah, I'm better at that!"

Later, as the toasts were nearly done, Kai gave one to her new wife.

"To Finley," she said, her glass held aloft, "my love, my life, thank you for everything you do every day for so many people. I know I speak for many here when I say that you've gotten us through this hellish year with so much support to those of us who needed it." Her gaze fell on Memphis, Harley, Wynter, Remi, all of whom nodded in agreement. "This year has been crap, I think that's safe to say, but ending it by becoming your spouse is definitely a highlight. Here's hoping 2021 is better."

Everyone held up their glasses, hoping against hope that 2021 was indeed better.

Due to Coronavirus (COVID-19), on Christmas Day 2020 there were:

2,209,620 Cases and 28,428 Deaths in California
80,393,607 Cases and 1,869,080 Deaths Worldwide

Epilogue

"Oh this sucks, this sucks so much…" Devin complained, as Skyler did her best to navigate the traffic that was back to near normal rates.

"I'm sorry, I'm sorry," Skyler chanted.

Devin was in labor, and even though Finley swore it was still going to be awhile, Skyler just wanted to get her wife to the hospital where she would be in better hands.

"What was I thinking?" Devin panted, as she did her best to breathe through a contraction.

"Babies are cute?" Skyler offered helpfully.

"This one better be!" Devin exclaimed as another contraction hit her.

While cases of Coronavirus were going down, California had just hit over 60,000 deaths—more than ten per cent of the national average. Regardless, Finley had promised that she'd be ready for Devin when they got there and that since Skyler and Devin had been in isolation for the last twenty days, she would let Skyler be with Devin in the delivery room. If they could just get there!

Six hours later, Fin Boché was born at six pounds, eight ounces. They'd named him after the woman that had gotten them all through the pandemic.

"I'm happy to announce that as of today anyone in the State that is age sixteen and over can get a vaccine," Midnight told the press. "I'm sincerely hoping that everyone in the State wants to do their part to end this pandemic and get back to normal. I know I'm sick to death of these!" She held her mask aloft making a face, causing the press to chuckle. "I know this has been a really tough road for all of us, but I think the State as a whole has done a great job of masking up and social distancing. Moving forward, I'm hoping to reopen the State fully in June. We got this people!"

Even as she said it, she knew there'd been dissention. She'd also just read a report that San Francisco was already seeing a variant of the virus that was a new mutant strain that may not be affected by the vaccine. She knew in her heart of hearts that neither the State nor the world was out of COVID-19's grip just yet. She sincerely hoped they would be someday in the near future. For now, she'd just do her best to roll with the punches and get her State through. She'd also already heard the grumblings about a Recall Election, she knew where that was coming from too.

She wasn't sure if the country would ever recover from the Trump administration, too many angry people had emerged from under their rocks, and it was likely they'd never fully get them back under. Racists and misogynists seemed to be coming out of the woodwork, goaded on by the former President's own statements and apparent mind set. With comments that called COVID the "China virus" or the "Kung flu" there'd been attacks on Asian-Americans in record numbers. With his snide comments about wearing masks, his supporters were constantly causing fights about being required to wear them. With comments about other options, like hydroxychloroquine or injecting disinfectant, he had people suspicious of vaccines. It was people like these that wanted her out of the Governor's seat.

Regardless, Midnight intended to do the best job possible for the citizens of the State. Even if she was removed as Governor, she'd continue, as she always had, to fight against people who would do others harm. She and her people would fight the pandemic until it was done and gone.

Acknowledgements

Thank you to my friend Tiffany Green for sharing her COVID story with me so I could put a real-life experience in the book! Glad everything worked out and you are well and thank you for the first-hand information!

You can find more information about the author and other books in the *WeHo* series here:

www.sherrylhancock.com
www.facebook.com/SherrylDHancock
www.vulpine-press.com/we-ho

Also by Sherryl D. Hancock:

The *MidKnight Blue* series. Dive into the world of Midnight Chevalier and as we follow her transformation from gang leader to cop from the very beginning.

www.vulpine-press.com/midknight-blue-series

The *Wild Irish Silence* series. Escape into the world of BJ Sparks and discover how he went from the small-town boy to the world-famous rock star.

www.vulpine-press.com/wild-irish-silence-series

CPSIA information can be obtained
at www.ICGtesting.com
Printed in the USA
LVHW032018270222
712155LV00002B/108

9 781839 191862